I0595032

Dedicated to YOU, my readers.

Don't let someone else's insanity become your love.
Move the obstropolous along.
They've already served their purpose.
You saw who they truly were to begin with.

- Eleonora Thomas

CONTENTS

NUT FREE

An Italian's way of dealing
with the disturbed

Eleonora Thomas

NUT FREE

Copyright © 2020 by Eleonora Thomas

The moral right of Eleonora Thomas to be identified as the author of this work has been asserted.

All rights reserved. No part of this publication may be reproduced, stored in or introduced into a retrieval system or distributed, or transmitted in any form or by any means, including photocopying, recording, or other electronic or mechanical methods, without the prior written permission of the copyright owner of this book.

This is a work of fiction. Names, characters, places, and incidents either are the product of the author's imagination or are used fictitiously. Any resemblance to actual persons, living or dead, events, or locales is entirely coincidental. Names, characters, and places are products of the author's imagination.

For information contact: Eleonora Thomas Author

Illustrations copyright ©

Cover design and typeset by Green Avenue Design

Editor Bianca Iovino

Proof reader Kristen Matisan

Unless otherwise indicated, scripture quotation is taken from:

Holy Bible, New International Version®, NIV® Copyright ©1973, 1978, 1984, 2011 by Biblica, Inc.® Used by permission. All rights reserved worldwide.

A catalogue record for this book is available from the National Library of Australia

ISBN: (Paperback) 978-0-6487257-1-8

Imprint: Independently Published

First Edition 2020

INTRODUCTION

Some believe love is a magical cure and the gateway to forgiveness. I'm here to tell you this universal four-letter word is often misused and overused. Some use this word as a lame excuse to dodge bad behaviour. We all need recognition and affirmation of love to survive. Love could be as simple as saying someone's name. So empowering, although so small, the positive reaction could be infectious. Love is an action, love is a gift. If you truly love someone you invest in that love. Love is showing gratitude for what you have. It's when you give your whole self to the relationship.

I'm Emanuela Smith, Emmie for short. I'm Italian and therefore I love hard. I love my food, I love my family, I love my friends and I love my life. I thought my upbringing was nuts, but in fact it was the opposite, it was real. I was taught to embrace authenticity. I try to avoid anything that is not healthy for me so I keep away from the artificial as best as I can.

I have food sensitivities and I am allergic to MSG, mostly found in Asian cuisine and anything else artificial. I'm here to tell you: bullshit to love conquering all and heartache being a universal lesson. Who wants to experience that kind of gripping pain? I've learnt to dodge heartache like my food intolerances. By being a better person and setting boundaries. Without boundaries you'll forever be chasing your tail.

Some say heartache makes you stronger in the long run. Through your journey in life, experiencing pain will lead you to self-discovery. You will ultimately find your strength and resilience and learn the art of forgiveness along the way. What we put out there, we are inevitably asking for in return.

It takes more strength and resilience to walk away from toxic relationships than what it does to stay. The staying bit is easy, you become accustomed to poor behaviour and in return you will start to project some of that yourself, you even begin to justify it. It will drive you crazy.

I like to think I am a generous, kind hearted person and I am not a hard nut to crack. I was raised to see the nice side of people. I was raised with a moral compass. But there are some people that are not so nice. I have found this group hard to define other than predators.

Like Italian almond biscotti, I could really do some damage trying to eat one without softening it first with espresso coffee. I mean, I like my two front teeth and wouldn't compromise them for a biscuit, so why would I compromise my sanity for someone who doesn't have my best interests at heart?

There are people who will try to entice you with rock hard biscotti. Pretending to be soft and fluffy on the inside. Choose these relationships wisely and listen carefully for empty promises. Sometimes you need to rely on more than just common sense. Should you find yourself at a crossroad of confusion: take your time, find your middle ground and listen to your instincts. Listen to what they're feeding you. You'll know when you're a priority and not just a passing fling.

Engage with healthy company, it saves lots of pain and perhaps even your two front teeth.

If you are in a relationship that does not allow compromise, their way or the highway, take the highway and run. Without compromise in any relationship you will be open to control and manipulation.

If someone causes you extreme pain, cuts you off at the knees and walks away without flinching, there will come a time they may also experience the same pain they caused you.

Perhaps they will try and justify it, but a loveless relationship is graded by a spectrum. Some are just out for themselves and will never truly understand or experience genuine love. They will be forever looking for something that does not exist. Refrain from owning other people's bad behaviour. Be aware when others prey on your vulnerabilities. Engage with people who fill you with complete trust.

At the end of the day, it comes back to your values. Stick with them and don't compromise them. Act with the highest integrity. People often forget this textbook lesson: treat others how you would like to be treated. I prefer not to leave a situation worse than I found it.

Italians are renowned for being dramatic and good knife throwers. I prefer to keep my silverware next to my plate when I eat, not in someone's chest or back.

There are lessons in life for all of us. If closure is not given, slam that door shut yourself and burn that bridge. There are always better things waiting around the corner. Stop wasting precious time seeking answers from someone who is already long gone. The only way is forward.

Broken hearts heal, but the brain is a little more complex. The in-betweens while they catch up to each other are lessons. I have mastered the art of listening to my gut when I am fighting between my head and my heart, even when I'm hungry.

I've learnt to keep my actions and thoughts real and responsible. Heartache comes and goes, but letting it happen over and over drags you into a sticky pattern. I've learnt many lessons and I've moved the fuck on. Those who don't will ultimately go nuts and drag those around them under too. I want to be the best person I can be: nut-free.

CHAPTER 1

JAM IS NOT SAUCE

I LIKED DATING Dave Smith. I wasn't allowed to date as a teenager. I was raised in an Italian household and boys weren't permitted. Dave was different, in a nerdy kind of way. He looked at life differently too. He knew a good thing when he saw it. His blue eyes were enticing and his appearance always neat. He had brown short hair. He took pride in his hairstyle going to the same barber each fortnight just like he did as a child. He had a kind, gentle way about him, he was genuine.

When Dave proposed, I was allowed out with him once a week until midnight. That was when we were engaged, not before. The before bit consisted of Dave and I watching television with my mother sitting in between us, until it was time for Dave to go home at 9 o'clock. My parents had rules I had to follow despite my age. Bless Dave for seeing the Italian dating process through. Maybe my mother was right, a way to a man's heart is through his stomach. Dave loved his pasta, so I guess that's one of the reasons why he stuck around.

"Emmie, we've been invited to Andy's girlfriends house for dinner Friday night," Dave said.

"We finally get to meet the new woman in his life, do we?" I asked.

"Yes, they've been dating for a few months now. Apparently, she's a musician and she plays the recorder. Andy was filling me in at footy practice the other night," he said.

"Really? I wouldn't think a musician playing the recorder was Andy's type. He's so quiet and shy. I wonder what she's like. Do you know how they even met?" I asked.

"He told me he went to an art fair with his mum and this woman handed him her flyer for recorder lessons. They got talking and he asked her out for coffee, other than that I don't really know much more, she's been a bit of a mystery. He hasn't even told me her name. I get the feeling his parents don't like her much, because Andy seems to spend more time at her place than at home," Dave said.

Andy Marks and Dave went to primary school together. I felt a little sorry for Andy. Out of all the friends in Dave's social group most were married or engaged except for Andy. He had always struggled meeting girls. He liked sitting in his bedroom tinkering with old typewriters, fixing them and replacing the ribbons then reselling them. He found interacting with girls difficult, as he was a shy and reserved man. Andy lived with his parents in a modest '70s cream brick home in the suburbs. Other than going to watch the occasional footy match with Dave he didn't really go out at all. He seemed a little socially inept.

"I'll pick you up Friday night at 6 o'clock," Dave said to me.

I was looking forward to meeting Andy's girlfriend. I liked making new friends and some of the girls in the friendship group were a little bitchy and competition seemed high amongst them. I didn't really care, I was happy to go out and spend time with Dave rather than sitting at home watching television with my parents.

Dave was so respectful, he would always have me back home on time when we went out together. He would call me Cinderella and if he didn't have me home by midnight I'd turn into a pumpkin and we would both laugh. His mates were very accepting of me.

I was happy for Andy. He finally managed to meet someone. It got him out of his bedroom and away from his typewriters. He was in a grown-up relationship with someone who he could hang out with other than Dave and me. We had only recently ditched my mother once we got engaged, but inherited Andy instead. We could now plan double dates, instead of him third wheeling with us.

When we arrived at Andy's girlfriend's house, I was surprised. It didn't look like a home that belonged to someone in their early 20's. She had the same pot plants out the front as my mother did. Large potted pink camellias and purple hydrangeas shielded from the sun with umbrellas. She grew herbs out the front just like my mother did too. I spotted parsley and rosemary growing by the fence.

"Dave have you ever met this woman before?" I asked, as we got out of the car.

"Em, I don't even know her name," he said, taking me by my hand.

As we walked up the driveway, I noticed she had a white birdbath in the middle of the front garden. I could see it had a little water in it and the bowl was stained with green algae. A wind-chime hanging from the front verandah blowing in the breeze caught my attention. It had a big blue butterfly on the top where the chimes dangled from the wings.

We had no sooner knocked and Andy opened the front door to greet us. I sensed his uneasiness.

Andy was a stocky build, short with thinning light brown hair. His eyes looked like strokes of water colour paints in pastel blue. Whenever I hugged him, he reminded me of my fluffy koala bear I had as a child. Warm and cuddly.

"Hi guys! Welcome, come in, come meet Jan," Andy said as he kissed me on the cheek.

I handed Andy a bottle of wine.

Jan's house smelt like lavender potpourri, it reminded me of my mother's linen cupboard. She would put sachets of lavender in amongst the towels and sheets to keep the moths at bay.

There was an old looking sofa covered in frayed rugs. There were statues of Buddha scattered around the room and spiritual prayer flags hanging from the doorway into the dining room.

Then I spotted them. The hairs on the back of my neck stood up as did theirs, Siamese cats. I hated cats. I couldn't stand cats. Hidden behind the sofa I saw three of them. At first, I thought it was only one, but then I saw the other two peering nearby.

I moved closer to Andy. "Andy, cats make me nervous! I don't like them," I said, grabbing him by the arm.

I could sense they were just as nervous as I was. Cats were drawn to me like some black cat to a witch. I simply did not cope in their presence. I began to wonder where Jan was. Couldn't she lock them in another room?

"Don't worry Em, just ignore them. They don't like visitors, they'll leave you alone," Andy said, not filling me with much confidence.

Great, I thought to myself. I didn't have a good feeling about this evening and the cats were the sign that confirmed it.

Jan walked out from the kitchen. The look on Dave's face must be the kind of look poor Andy gets each time he introduces Jan. No wonder he took his time acquainting her with his mates. I had to act quickly and think on my feet.

I stepped towards her. "Jan pleased to meet you. Thank you for inviting us over for dinner," I said, giving her an awkward hug.

It felt like the sort of hug I'd give to Dave's alcoholic aunt after one of her regular falls. The type that lack any real sincerity, but did it anyway out of obligation and politeness.

Jan was in her mid-fifties. Not that there's anything wrong with dating someone older, but she did not suit Andy. Jan was wearing a long patchwork velvet dress. She wore a thickly cabled, hand-knitted pink cardigan over the top. Her hair was a combination of leftover brassy colour with different shades of grey amongst it, tied up in a messy bun. She had bulging brown eyes that looked like the type you would find on pop eye goldfish. She smelt like my mother did when she overused talcum powder after a shower.

Jan was softly spoken. I had to concentrate to hear her at first, causing my face to frown.

Andy was trying hard to break the ice and, in the process, he nearly broke his leg. Falling over a plastic milk crate that was left sitting in the middle of the lounge room.

I jumped, "Andy are you okay?" I asked, rushing over to help him.

Dave was still standing in the same spot from when we had arrived. He wasn't good at small talk and meeting Jan had really thrown him off guard. He still looked like he was in a state of surprise.

Jan rushed over. "That's my office!" she exclaimed.

Dave and I looked around the room, we were both confused. Did she mean the lounge room was her office?

Jan walked over to the plastic milk crate and picked it up.

"This is my office," she proudly said waving the blue crate high in the air.

"Jan sits on this crate at various fairs when she plays her recorder," Andy jumped in to explain.

"Oh," I said, sounding confused.

Jan proudly said, "Yes, I play the recorder. I like playing old English folk tunes mostly," as she dragged out a box full of the obnoxious things.

Looking at Jan's recorders instantly brought back memories of my music lessons in high school. Memories I would rather forget.

I disliked the recorder as much as I disliked cats. I was forced to play it in high school. I remembered how I wanted to play the clarinet, but the music teacher, Mrs Silvorski said I had to learn the recorder first. I began to think of the staunch Polish woman who taught music at that all girls' Catholic school. One day when I went to her lesson where she continued to criticise my playing technique, I told her where she could stick her recorder. She didn't take kindly to my suggestion and locked me in the soundproof practice room. She conveniently forgot about me. The cleaner, Mrs Brown had to let me out. Stupid Mrs Silvorski and her brown recorders. That so-called musical instrument had left an unimpressionable scar.

Jan sifted through her box and pulled out a wooden brown recorder. She sat high on her crate and she began to play. I looked over at Andy who was trying his best to normalise the awkwardness amongst us. I then looked over at Dave who looked at me with his bright blue eyes. He felt uncomfortable and I couldn't blame him.

The cats stirred under the sofa, one jumped out from the back and ran into another room. I jumped to one side bumping into Dave. I was anxious and none of this made any sense to me. What the fuck was Andy thinking? This woman was in another world engrossed by her own music making.

Jan had belted out more tunes on her plastic magic instrument than any other musician on the Eurovision contest I had watched on television the night before.

"Jan," Andy said loudly enough to be heard over her music.

"I think we should open the wine our guests have brought, and would you like me to check on dinner?"

Jan got up, put her recorder away and led us to the dining room table.

She insisted we take a seat. "Please sit," she said.

"I've made my specialty, apricot chicken."

"Jan makes the best apricot chicken," Andy praised her.

I elbowed Dave sitting next to me. I had never eaten apricot chicken before. Italians didn't eat this type of food and it didn't sound appealing.

Jan was talking about her latest psychic fair that she was going to be playing at and how intuitive she was. She had spent time in Nepal developing her spirituality. She was able to read people and offer them insight into their futures. I wondered whether she was as intuitive as she said because this woman was doing my head in. Between her cats jumping about and her music making, I just wanted to go home.

"Dinner is served," Andy said, as he placed the plate in front of me.

He smiled and looked proudly down at the plate of food.

I looked down at the orange blob. It looked like someone had tipped a whole jar of apricot jam on a plate and sprinkled crushed peanuts on top. I couldn't see the chicken. I liked apricot jam, my mother made her own. We would spread it on our bread, not over our chicken.

I took my knife and scraped the jam off the top. I politely cut into the meat and put a tiny bit in my mouth. It tasted awful. Jan, who seemed to be quiet and mousy at first, was now dominating the table conversation. I looked up at Andy sitting nervously opposite me. I elbowed Dave again, he looked down at his plate and we had the same thought, no crystal ball or psychic required, we both wanted out.

Italians loved their food, in fact there really wasn't much I didn't like eating. Growing up I had been fed lots of different and wonderful dishes. Some were force fed. Others, I couldn't get enough of. In this case I simply could not eat Jan's apricot chicken.

As a young adult, this woman was my first taste of a real nut that I recognised upon meeting. Past nuts I had met took time for a reaction to occur, this one was immediate. There was something that didn't quite sit well with me from when I walked through her front door. I now understood why Andy's parents may also have an aversion to her too.

Part way through my meal I began to scratch my arms. I was scratching my head and my hands. I had to make something up fast to remove myself and Dave from this situation.

"Jan, Andy," I began to say.

I rolled the sleeves of my jumper. "I'm so sorry, but I'm highly allergic to cats, I can't stand it anymore, I'm really sorry, but I have to leave."

Dave pretended to understand, and went along with my act.

"Andy, mate, once she starts scratching, she can't stop. I'll have to get her home. I'll see you at footy training Wednesday night," Dave said as he got up from the table.

"I better get Em outside before she tears her jumper off. Thank you so much for dinner Jan. We will have to try for another time," Dave said.

Dave and I liked Andy, but Jan was not for him. She had her own place in this world as did he. For whatever reason their paths crossed I doubt their relationship would progress beyond her signature dish. Sometimes people meet in life to learn something from one another. Was it coincidental these people enter our lives or do they come to leave us with lessons? I had learnt there was no way I could spend another moment with Jan. I had also discovered Dave and I were on the same page. We wanted to leave behind a situation that made us both feel uncomfortable. Although Jan seemed like a harmless nut, we didn't want to be around her. I loved Dave Smith so much. I couldn't wait to start my life with him. I could finally start living. Married life was going to be straightforward and uncomplicated. Our life was going to be perfect and nut free.

CHAPTER 2

EVEN NICE NUTS CAUSE HIVES

Growing up in the '70s wasn't easy. I was an Italian raised in Australia. Although I was born in Australia, I was labelled according to my ethnicity. Especially when the main language spoken at home was Italian. My parents didn't understand pie floaters or Australian slang.

People could be mean. But my parents taught me to be patient and mean people would eventually move on.

"Look for the good in them instead," they'd say.

"Do the right thing by others and you'll be fine," they'd say.

I had developed my life saving skills from a very young age known as strength and resilience. I hadn't met my instincts yet. These would come later.

I thought my parents were crazy. I'd make up stories in my mind of one day making my grand escape, or perhaps someone would abduct me and take me away. I even went snooping for documents that my father kept safely in an old shoe box, hoping to find something to prove I was in fact adopted. Then I could tell myself the insanity they displayed wasn't running through my veins as well.

My household consisted of strong family values and an even stronger religious faith. If you were 'good', then nothing 'bad' would happen to you. If you followed the rules and you were kind to others, then life would be kind to you.

At times, I found this hard to digest because my parents would yell at one another a fair bit for no reason. My father

Gino Sopracasa moved to Australia when he was 18 years old and my mother Ida Sopracasa soon followed.

My father and I had the same green eyes and fair skin. He had a well chiselled jawline. He was always smartly dressed and wore a navy-blue woollen herringbone flat cap.

My father was a builder. According to him, he used real bricks and not brick veneer. What he meant was, he would build double brick homes. It didn't matter if they would eventually crack in twenty years' time because of the soil conditions, it had to be double brick.

My father built the house we lived in. It was on a main road so everyone could see what an amazing builder he was. We had large white pillars out the front. We had fruit trees and flowers growing in the garden.

As a young child I was forced to sit on a wooded box on the front footpath and sell Mother's Day flowers my father grew. Bunches of different coloured chrysanthemum sitting in plastic buckets. It was only through an unfortunate experience I had encountered with a customer I was allowed to stop selling them. On this day the customer was topless and wearing loose running shorts. He came up to pay when I noticed part of his lower anatomy hanging out one side of his shorts. It was virtually down to his knee. I tried to do the right thing and wrap his flowers in newspaper, but he scared me and I ran inside. My mother chased him down the road waving her shoe in the air. I felt bad for not serving him, but he was too disgusting for my liking.

My mother took pride in her appearance and was immaculately dressed. She wore bright red lipstick. She took as much pride in her home as she did with her hair styles. She had dark hair that matched her soft brown eyes. She would have it styled every Saturday morning by a hairdresser.

She cleaned at the local hospital where she spent most of her time socialising instead of working.

I learnt from a very young age to take care of myself. I was an only child. I didn't have any hand holding to and from school. I got myself there and back, rain, hail or shine. With my school bag and piggy tails swinging side to side.

My parents hid the house key out in the back shed in an old metal ice-cream tin so I could let myself in each afternoon. I liked my alone time. I enjoyed reading, and my imaginary friends were my companions.

I was expected to attend church each Sunday with my parents. Sometimes I would listen to the mass and other times I would become so bored I would study the different variety of soles on people's shoes when kneeling to pray. I did have a strong faith, I liked praying, and having someone other than my parents to talk to and share my secrets with was a good thing. My mother had a way of guilting me into telling her everything and then punishing me if she didn't like what she heard.

My parents had religious portraits everywhere in their home. From the Last Supper hanging up in the dining room to the holographic crucifixion hanging up in the hallway, I was taught very early on to be good. I did not want to be nailed to a wooden cross. As confronting as these pictures may have been to others, depicting the pain Jesus must have endured in his final hours, to me it represented strength.

Father Vincent was our local Italian priest. He would have lunch with us most Sundays after mass.

"Emanuela! Get the tavolo (table) ready," my mother was yelling out to me.

"Sbrigati (hurry up)," she said.

My mother had two kitchens. She used the outside kitchen as to not dirty the one inside. She would race back and forth juggling large pots of pasta whilst trying to open the back door. I would get an earful if I wasn't around to help her with her juggling act. She would blame me for not helping her when she needed me. I didn't understand why she couldn't cook inside and save us all the headache. She nearly burnt down the outside kitchen once. She had forgotten the fried capsicum on the stove top. I wished she had, but instead she put the fire out with her apron.

"Why does Father Vincent have to eat here again?" I'd ask her.

"Why do you prepare a feast for him each Sunday?"

"Emanuela, you have to respect a man of the church!" she'd say.

I found Sunday lunches boring. I wanted to go to my room and read, but instead I had to sit around the table listening to Father Vincent go on about the sacrifices he'd made in order to spread the word of God. I began to wonder that women probably made the most sacrifices in their lives. I was expected to clean and help my mother and follow in her footsteps. My role had already been predetermined from birth. I had a duty to uphold and that was to my family.

After each course my mother served, I would diligently clear their plates and put them in the kitchen sink ready to wash. She would make two courses, primo e secondo. We finished off with coffee and cake, usually a homemade rum baba cake filled with Italian custard and soaked in rum. Alcohol was used in lots of Italian deserts.

I liked Father Vincent. He was a gentle soul. He stood up for me and my father listened to him. He wouldn't dare question a man of the church. He spoke English quite well for an Italian priest. He was a handsome looking man dressed entirely in black with a white tab collar peeking through. He was young with light coloured hair and big brown eyes. He always wore the same aftershave. The scent reminding me of forest scented pinecones.

On this day, at the dining table, Father Vincent gave me a little wink before he spoke to my father.

"Gino let Emmie go and play. She looks lonely sitting here listening to us speak," he said after we had finished our lunch.

I immediately sat upright. Father Vincent could sense I was bored and lonely. I had washed all the dishes and had just sat back down. I was staring at the elaborately carved wooden display wall unit in the dining room. I was secretly counting all the bonbonnière my mother had collected over the years from all the parties we had attended. I was never allowed to eat the sugared almonds attached to them. Apparently, they were too pretty to eat. The different coloured nuts staring at me nestled in white nets tied with satin bows around porcelain figurines.

"Emanuela, have you finished helping your mother?" my father asked.

"Yes papà," I replied.

He knew I had finished helping my mother. She was sitting at the same table. *Why was he so annoying?*

He looked at me sternly, "Go play then," he said and I got up to leave.

My parents taught me never to be rude and to listen to grown-ups when they spoke. I had to be respectful to the adults I encountered in my life. Children were to be seen and not heard.

We lived next door to a nice old couple, Mr and Mrs King. When I was allowed, I would go visit them. Mrs King would offer me the best burnt butter biscuits I had ever eaten. She would bake them with a little blanched almond on top of each cookie, served neatly stacked on a fine bone china saucer. They were almonds straight from the trees they grew in their backyard. I liked helping Mr King in his garden. I'd help him pick almonds from his almond trees. I'd pick them and peel back the fury green skin and eat the kernel. In fact, I really enjoyed spending time with them, they didn't yell and they were always quiet and calm.

I didn't like the neighbours on the other side of our home. Even though my parents liked them because they were Italian, I didn't. I always had a funny feeling about Pina.

Pina Zappia had two older children from a previous marriage. Apparently, her ex-husband raised their children because of some mental health issues Pina had. There weren't too many divorced Italian women in the '70s. My mother said Pina was a nice lady regardless of her issues, and it was our duty to help women who came from troubled backgrounds. Sometimes Pina would have to spend time in a hospital and when she returned home my mother would check up on her and bring her food.

Pina would always ask me over and would want to make me dresses. She was a seamstress. She would tell me how she missed her boys but how she secretly had always wanted a little girl. I didn't feel comfortable around Pina, and I couldn't explain the funny feeling in my stomach each time I saw her either.

"Emanuela, go to Pina's house after school. She wants to make you a dress for your Holy Communion," my mother said.

"Ma, I don't want to go on my own, why can't you come with me?" I asked.

"Emanuela I don't have time, I have to work. Don't start trouble, vai!" she said, instructing me to go.

"I don't like Pina, ma."

"Perchè? Non fa la stupida, she's a very nice lady and you must be nice to her. She has made you lots of nice dresses," my mother said.

Pina had short curly black hair. She had a pasty white face and dark eyes, they almost looked black. She would wear short tight dresses with big bright flowers and high heels. Her husband was rarely home, and her house was always poorly lit. She never had the blinds up to let in sunlight. Each time I would go over it felt strange, not welcoming like Mr and Mrs King's home. They welcomed me going over, they were kind. I always felt that although Pina asked me over, I was an inconvenience to her. She didn't like it when I spoke or asked her questions. She would become agitated very quickly.

I was not looking forward to Pina making me another dress, but I didn't want my mother yelling at me for not going and then telling my father I didn't listen to her.

I was worried for most of the day at school knowing I had to go to Pina's for a fitting on my way home.

When I arrived, I knocked on Pina's door and waited for her to answer. I wanted this fitting over as quickly as possible so I could go home and watch afternoon cartoons.

She opened the door, "Emmie, come in, you can leave your school bag by the door," she instructed.

"Hello Pina, thank you," I said as I dropped my little bag on the ground and followed her into her sewing room.

"You know I am doing you and your mother a very big favour making this dress for you," she said.

"I don't understand why your mother couldn't buy you a dress?" she asked.

I was confused. My mother told me Pina had insisted on making my Holy Communion dress. My mother had the fabric sent over from Italy. When Pina saw the fabric, she had offered to sew it herself. She told my mother it was the most beautiful fabric she had ever seen.

She began to run her tape measure over my arm. "Stand still! You keep moving. I have to measure you," Pina said.

Then she put the tape measure across my hips, carefully taking the correct measurement and writing it down.

"I have to make a pattern and you are annoying me!" she angrily snapped.

I was patiently standing as she had instructed me to do so. Was this woman crazy? I began to have this funny feeling rise from the pit of my stomach, and it wasn't hunger pains. It felt like it was rising from deep within.

"OUCH!" I said.

Pina had stuck a pin into me.

"OUCH," and then another one.

"Stop being a naughty little girl! Bad things happen to naughty girls," Pina said.

"You stuck pins into me on purpose!" I said treading cautiously.

My fear set upon me and my heart began to pound.

"Don't be stupid, you're a liar!" she snapped back.

"No one will believe a stupid little girl like you."

Her eyes looked black. Like two dark endless pits in some faraway cemetery in the middle of the night. Her gaze looked like it was going to pierce my soul.

I saw Pina do it, she pricked me twice. I could feel my eyes watering up. I didn't move and Pina had stuck pins into me. I was frozen with uncertainty. The feeling in my stomach began speaking to my mind and it told me to get out of her house immediately. I had to plan my escape and that being a good girl to this crazy woman, was going to get me jabbed with only more pins. She had pins in her mouth most likely ready to strike again. Shiny, pointy metal coloured dressmaker pins.

Pina turned around to get more sewing pattern paper to measure on my back. I had paper pined to my arms. I turned around and ran to the front door. I felt the paper flapping on my arms. I left my school bag behind. I raced right up the driveway and into the back shed at home. I quickly grabbed the key out of the metal ice-cream tin and let myself in and locked the door behind me. I ran straight into my room and cried.

My mother arrived home shortly after.

"Emanuela! Che è successo? (What happened?)" she asked.

I told my mother what Pina had done and how I had left my school bag at her house. I was scared my mother was going to yell at me. I was still sobbing sitting on my bed. I cried so hard my pink and white handkerchief felt damp.

My mother left my bedroom without saying a word. I followed behind her and saw her take a broom out of the laundry cupboard. She told me to stay inside and watch television as she left.

I thought I heard a door slam and people yelling, but I was too scared to go outside. My mother had returned not long after with my school bag and her broom. She sat beside me and kissed me. She told me I would never have to be nice to people like Pina again. She explained that funny feeling I described to her was a sign from God called instincts. She said I did the right thing by running away from her. She also said that I will meet people who pretend to be nice but it's only to trick us before their mask falls.

When I took a closer look at my mother's broom, I noticed the broom head was missing and the wooded handle had a split in it. We never saw Pina again after that. My mother told me people like her deserve to live in the dark, crazy bitch.

CHAPTER 3

DOT POINTS

I ENJOYED SPENDING time with my mother and her friends. I liked listening to their stories they would share over coffee when they visited. I would sit at the kitchen table with them. I learnt a lot from their conversations. They were very smart, savvy women. My mother had a hard time conceiving me and she had me at forty years of age. Her friends had older children so they welcomed my presence. They liked having me around. I was the kid that had cute, chubby cheeks on the block.

Growing up, I was embarrassed my mother was a lot older than the other mothers the kids at school had. It wasn't often she would come to my school. When she did, I wanted to hide. She was very pretty, but the other mothers were a lot younger. They wore jeans and t-shirts. My mother wore designer Italian dresses. My mother didn't care what the Aussie modern women wore because she preferred to be a classic beauty instead.

School was hard for me. I was picked on, mainly because of my ethnicity. It didn't matter that I was born in Australia, my parents weren't Aussies. The other kids didn't understand I was just like them. I liked playing on the school playground as they all did. I liked watching the same television shows they did. I wanted to join in on their conversations also. I didn't have many friends because I was perceived as different. I was teased because of my name, the clothes I wore, the house I lived in and the food I ate. My mother didn't dress me in navy fleece wear. My dresses were made for me using Italian fabric my nonna would send over from Italy.

I tried making friends, but to little avail. Apparently, I was some disease infested foreigner no one wanted around. I was the kid who ate smelly lunches. I knew deep down they really feared me because I was perceived as different. I was known as a wog. I didn't really understand what that word meant, but I knew it was to label me. They didn't understand my cultural background. I didn't understand the difference between me and them. I thought we were all kids at school for the same reason, to learn and to have fun together.

I was happy to go to school and be left alone. I had no choice but to accept this. I chose happiness over loneliness. I would secretly laugh at the kids in class. The only subject I didn't like was sex education. It grossed me out, reminding me of the encounter I had with that werido when I was selling Mother's Day flowers and all the stupid naked statues my mother had on display at home.

I preferred maths and science. During lessons when the teacher would explain a scientific equation, I was always the first one to work it out. The others were all too busy pretending not to listen, so they didn't have to apply themselves. They were lazy, I wasn't. I liked a challenge and learning helped fill my void of loneliness. I didn't have much else I was allowed to do. I wasn't allowed to play weekend sports or have a hobby. My parents were too busy with their own lives to drive me around. Reading became my hobby. I was raised to work hard and reap the rewards later.

School was changing with the times and diversity was slowly being introduced and acknowledged. We were having International Food Day and we all had to bring a dish from our cultural background.

My one and only friend, Rani Ashini had not long arrived from India and lived locally. I was happy when she started school. She didn't have friends either. She was teased because of her white teeth. I asked her about her teeth once. She told me she used a mixture of charcoal and baking soda. My father would never let me use charcoal. He said it was only Greeks that used it.

We were in year 7 in our final year at primary school. I was going to miss Rani. She was going to a mixed high school. My father had enrolled me at an all-girls Catholic school. Apparently as a girl, I would go on to develop hormones and my father didn't want me mixing with boys.

"Rani what are you bringing? What is your mum going to make?" I asked.

"My mum is making samosa," she said.

Rani had jet-black hair down to her waist, and the whitest teeth I had ever seen on a person. She was tiny and petite. She was like me, we both liked to read books, and we would both hide in the school library to avoid being teased by the other kids.

"What is your mum making Emmie?" she asked.

"She's making stuffed capsicum," I replied.

"I wish she would just make a spaghetti frittata so it can be cut up into little pieces. Now I'll be teased for these big fat red things. Dripping in oil and smelling like garlic, she insisted on making," I said and we both giggled.

My mother was a great cook, but this time I wished she would make something simple. Stuffed capsicums were hard to eat, and I doubted the Aussie kids even ate capsicum at all. She claimed these weren't for the kids, these were for the teachers. She thought they would have a better appreciation for them.

Times were changing at school and so were the teachers. We had an Italian teacher who taught English.

I didn't like our English teacher, Mr Grazzio, much. He was the same age as my mother. He had shiny, olive coloured skin, and a round face. His hair was always combed back which made him look even slicker. His skin produced enough oil to dress a salad. He wore shirts and would leave the top buttons undone, allowing the masses of black chest hair to peek out the top. He had hairy arms, reminding me of a bear. He wore tight denim flared jeans and during class I would hope to God the top button didn't pop off each time he sat down.

When he would spot me out in the school yard he would run up and ask me about my mother. He said she had class and grace. I guess I associated class and grace with Gina Lollobrigida. She was my inspiration and my idol. He was always asking me if my mother could go in and speak with him about my English classes. He would have the biggest smile on his face each time she did. My mother found him annoying because she didn't have time to come to my school. She didn't see a need for meaningless discussions especially when I was an A grade student. She told me once she was there for his benefit and not mine, but I didn't understand what she had meant.

Walking to school holding a tray of stuffed capsicums and my school bag was no easy task. They weighed a tonne. By the time I had arrived my arms felt like they had been in a torturous Chinese burn.

I was walking across the school yard making my way to class.

Mr Grazzio spotted me, "Emmie, what have you got there?" he asked as he approached me.

"My mother made stuffed capsicum for International Food Day," I replied.

"I think she made those for me," he said as he winked at me and walked off.

I don't think so Mr Grazzi-hairy-arse, I thought to myself.

I knew Mr Grazzio thought my mother was pretty. His face would turn cherry red when she came to speak to him at parent-teacher interviews. His body language would change each time he saw her. He would sit up-right and run his hands through his oily hair. He became nice and kind, not grumpy and he pretended to like me. He even smiled at me once.

"Ma, I think my teacher likes you," I said after she had come to class to speak with him.

"Yes, Emanuela, I know he does," she said.

"How do you know, ma?" I asked surprised.

"Because men aren't good at hiding how they feel about women. He has good taste," she giggled.

She saw the look on my face. I was shocked my mother was having this sort of discussion with me. This was the sort of conversation she would share with her friends instead.

"Emanuela, your teacher is a nice man. He likes pretty women, but most of all he likes confident women because they are the ones that make his heart beat fast and make him feel nervous. I know you wished I was like the other mothers, but I'm not. Sometimes that makes me sad because I like who I am, and I wish you did too. I will not pretend to be someone I'm not. I'm not perfect, but I know where my heart lies. I might be loud at times and fight with your father because he annoys me, but I do care for him and for you. You probably don't believe me, but I do," she said.

"Mr Grazzio is mean to me in class," I said.

"He is a teacher, he's there to teach. He probably likes talking to the mothers, it's a distraction from his day, and there is nothing wrong with that. I am married to your father. You have nothing to worry about with Mr Grazzio. A good relationship is when you accept people for who they are. You support each other and work together, not against one another. Do you think your father built a business on his own? He had me by his side. I ran the household, while he ran the business. I raised you so he could work. I wasn't the only one who wanted a baby, he did too," she said.

"I have met many men in my life just like Mr Grazzio, he is a persona innocua (harmless person). Emanuela you too will meet men one day, don't be fooled by the ones who sweep you off your feet and make empty promises. Love is what someone feels, but it should also be someone's actions. When you love someone, you treat them with respect and trust, there should be no jealousy, and there should be affection. Love makes you feel safe and protected, and when you do encounter problems, you resolve them together not avoid them. Don't be fooled by those who will use it to reward or punish you, that is not love," she said.

"Is love like Rock Hudson and Gina Lollobrigida?" I asked.

She smiled, "You will know what love is when you find it. Be smart, not stupida, some men wear masks."

I thought of our old nut-job neighbour Pina, my mother once told me she wore a mask too.

I looked at her strangely, "What masks? Like the ones the men wear during Carnevale?" I asked.

She laughed, "Si, like those masks, they pretend to be someone they are not. Due facce (two faced). They will be nice to other people, but not nice when they are behind closed doors. They come from blame and will never admit any wrongdoing, they will try to control you. They will look at others, or even want to be with them and then say it's because of you. They will act superior and not let you have friends or see your family. They will lie to your face."

"Ma, I'm scared. I want to meet someone nice when I grow up. I don't know if I will be able to recognise these people."

"Scared? Perchè?" she asked.

"Emanuela, you will get to know people and if anyone hurts you, I'll snap them in half and then I'll spit on them!" she exclaimed.

"You have nothing to fear in life but fear itself."

At that very moment I realised, I had experienced my first grown up conversation with my mother. Just like the ones she had with her friends. This was only one conversation and advice I would have to remember to carry with me. *Emmie don't forget this*, I thought to myself. *My mother is always right.*

CHAPTER 4

My MOTHER WAS a great planner. She would always pre-plan her meals for special occasions. Easter and Christmas were something to look forward to. Food was exceptional in an Italian household. What we ate depended on what was in season. Fat was considered healthy and the word diet didn't exist. I was told as a child if I ever became unwell, I had enough fat stored on my body to help me recover. I had visions of skinny, but this was not allowed.

Special occasions had special types of food. Pizza piena for Easter was an expectation to have. It was made according to the Italian region you came from, there were slightly different versions of the same dish. She would bake her amazing pie on Good Friday and make us wait an entire 24 hours before we could eat it. It was a sin to eat meat on Good Friday and pizza piena was full of small-goods. The wait to bite into a warm slice was agonising.

Some foods had the ability to cause real childhood trauma. I was made to eat different foods whether I wanted to or not, I wasn't given a choice. According to my parents, food gave you strength. Strength to get you through what life served you. I needed strength, especially at Christmas time, but not from certain dishes I was fed.

"Ida, hurry up, we have to go buy anguilla (eels) before they all sell out." I heard my father call out to my mother.

"Hurry up Emanuela, you can come too," he said.

"I don't want to come. I want to stay home," I said.

"Get in the car with your mother," he instructed.

Going to buy live eels for Christmas Eve dinner was embarrassing. It wasn't something I wanted to be a part of. We would go to the local supermarket where they had a large tank in the shopping centre car park full of slippery black sea creatures. My parents would buy a bag full and put them in the boot of the car in a large plastic tub. I was fascinated at how the black sea snakes were caught by the shopping attendant and quickly shoved into a plastic bag. Who'd want a job doing that? Poor guy probably wished he was pushing trolleys out in the hot sun or serving intolerable Christmas crazed customers at a checkout instead.

I'd question my parents why it was always so important to them that food had to be fresh? Their version of fresh was still alive and kicking. I never understood why they couldn't go buy eels that were already prepared ready for cooking from a seafood shop. My poor mother was expected to prepare these things in order to feed my father.

"Only the best is fresh," he'd say.

When we arrived home, my mother would release the eels into the laundry trough partially filled with water. It was times like these I wished she had a second laundry outside. She had two of everything else. Each time I would open the laundry door I'd find something different in there. If it wasn't buckets of lupini beans soaking, it would be bucket's full of olives, or salted baccalà fish soaking in tubs of water.

The black squirmy snakes swam about happily not knowing what loomed. I couldn't watch my mother grab them as they would squirm in her hands. I tried once, but hid in my room instead, and I tried not to let my imagination get the better of me. If I watched her, I would dream of snakes for weeks.

My mother was like a fearless warrior with her sharp, shiny, silver, scissors and pretty apron. She would get to work and clean them promptly. In no time at all, they were filleted and laid out on a tray, ready for the frypan.

"Ma, aren't you scared?" I'd ask her.

"No! Emanuela, in life you must be in control, if something or someone senses you are scared, they will turn on you. Remember this, va bene?" she said making sure I understood.

"Even if you have to pretend for a brief moment, believe in yourself that you can do it and take back control," she said.

"Okay ma, I understand. But I'm not eating eels for dinner!" I said.

Sauce day was an international family gathering. It was like planning an Italian wedding. It involved a group of skilled family members coming together on a hot summer day. We'd spend the day sweltering over tomatoes floating in hot boiling water and trying not to kill one another. There would no doubt be threats of schiaffi (slaps) left, right and centre, if we weren't following instructions. The day usually ended with a big feast of food made from the freshest sauce and famished angry Italians wiping their plates clean, using soft thickly sliced continental bread. It was an event like no other. It required a group effort and a great deal of patience and compromise.

My parents would make their own tomato sauce each year. My father would spend weeks sourcing only the best organic roma tomatoes to be used. He would travel to all the market gardens north of the city searching for only the sweetest, reddest and ripest, where he would buy boxes full.

Once he got them home, he would have the boxes lined up in the back shed and covered with linen sheets in preparation for the big day. I would watch him check on his boxes each morning. He would tenderly hold up a few tomatoes from each box and look at them and smile to himself. At times I wished he put the same amount of nurturing into me like he did with his tomatoes.

The hot summer day had been set and locked in. My cousins were coming to help with their parents. I had three cousins, Rosie, Renata and her older sister Maria. Renata and Maria Sopracasa are my cousins on my father's side. Rosie Santino is my cousin on my mother's side. Maria was a lot older. We were told Renata was conceived in error. Apparently, her mother had one too many vinos one night. Italians saying like it was, there were never any secrets amongst family members. Maria was seventeen years older than Renata. Maria drove her mother home from the hospital with the newborn in tow because my then uncle had to work.

We each had our own tasks and workstations for sauce day. Renata had to wash each recycled glass beer bottle and lay them in a row on the backyard lawn. She was always getting tangled up in the garden hose.

I oversaw the picking and washing of all the basil leaves. I had to put them in the bottles ready for the sauce to go in. Rosie would have to wash all the bottle tops ready to place on each bottle once the sauce had been poured into them. It was like an assembly line in an Italian factory, knowing the finished product would go on to make the best food dishes.

Renata was always trying to get out of helping. She stood up from laying out all the empty beer bottles.

She wiped her perspiration from her forehead, "It's so bloody hot today, isn't it illegal to light a fire to cook the bottles of sauce?" she asked.

She was wearing a blue t-shirt with a peace sign on it. Her hair was tied back, and her pale face seemed to make her green eyes stand out.

"As if our parents care, they have over three hundred bottles they have to cook before any of us can leave," Rosie replied.

Rosie had her hair tied back in a neat bun. We weren't allowed to wear our long hair down around food preparation. Our mothers would make us tie it up and put on an apron before we entered the kitchen. I was surprised they didn't make us wear plastic shower caps like they had in the past.

"Shut up Renata, if my mum hears you complaining about the heat, she'll make us go sit in the cellar to cool off," I said.

My father had a concrete cellar in his shed where he would store all his wine and jars of food. It was always cold in there. It was more like a dark concreted hole in the ground where the only way in and out was to climb an old ladder. On hot days my mother would make me and my cousins sit in there to cool off so she didn't have to turn the air conditioner on.

"I'm not in the mood to sit in a dark hole surrounded by dusty jars of olives," I said.

I continued to put the washed basil leaves in the colander. I was wearing denim shorts and a checkered short sleeve shirt tied up at the front. My skin and hair smelt like firewood, the smoke travelling from the fire under the cauldron.

"I think we have to take it in turns to watch the fire under the cauldron," Rosie said.

"Emanuela, where's your apron?" my mother asked. "And put your shoes on, you'll catch a cold!"

It was forty degrees celsius and Renata didn't wear shoes. She was always walking barefoot. I rolled my eyes at my cousins and ignoring her, I went back to putting basil leaves in bottles.

"I like the feeling of wet grass beneath my feet on a hot day," I said under my breath.

"Mamma mia, have you changed religion? Put your shoes on!" she barked.

She bent down and looked at the sauce bottles I had lined up on the lawn.

"Emanuela, put more basil in those bottles!"

I wish she didn't have to check up on every task I was asked to do. She reminded me of a supervisor inspecting my work, micromanaging my every move. She had the perfectionist gene that I gladly missed out on.

My parents had the biggest blackest cauldron that could potentially fit a small child in. It reminded me of something that a witch would use to cook in. Just like Strega Nona did in the children's book I still had sitting on my bookshelf in my room.

They would pack it full of the bottled sauce and cook them slowly over an open fire in their backyard. There was a process to all of this in order to produce the best sauce possible. They weren't going to compromise their sauce because of the weather. The tomatoes were already perfectly ripe. They had to be used on time. They had a job to see through.

It was never easy on sauce day without a fight breaking out. In fact, when it came to my father and gatherings there were always fights breaking out. We watched carefully for which parent would unhinge first. If it wasn't between my parents, it would be between Rosie's parents. Everyone seemed to have a better way of doing things. Suggestions weren't taken on board easily and opinions were scoffed at.

But it was my father who would have the ultimate say. Or so he thought.

"Gino, put more wood in the fire, it will burn out!" my mother instructed my father, standing with her hands on her hips. Her lime green apron had pink splatters all over it.

"It doesn't need any yet," he replied.

"Si, it does!" she snapped.

My father was trying to ignore her, and she would repeat what she had asked him to do. Over, and over again until he gave in and before the insults started to fly.

We watched my father put more wood in the fire.

As the day wore on everyone began to show signs of irritability, but he ran his international sauce show. We had to follow his instructions. And he had no problems when it came to delegating them.

"Add more salt!" I heard my aunt instruct my father.

"No! Adesso basta! (Enough!)" he'd say.

My cousins and I stopped what we were doing and looked at one another. *Here we go.* It was on. A fight was about to break out. By now my father looked like he had enough of being told how and what to do. He looked tired and annoyed. His brown checkered shirt had sauce splattered all over it. His forehead had beads of perspiration glistening in the sun.

"You need more sala (salt) in the sauce," my aunt repeated.

"I said NO!" my father barked.

He began to curse in Italian under his breath to various Saints. Even my dog, Rocky who was nearby sensed my father's anger rising and ran to hide in his kennel.

"Ma perchè? (Why?)" she asked dramatically throwing her hands up in the air.

"It needs more salt!"

They were facing each other, a deadlock between two opponents. My father was tired and hot and my aunt who was annoyed and hungry. We were waiting to see who was going to fly off the handle first.

And then it happened, all three of us stood and watched in amazement. My father walked over to the salt jar and grabbed a handful. He tossed it into the sauce that was ready to be poured into the empty bottles.

"Okay we try your way, but we will add small amounts as we go," he huffed.

My aunt smiled. She had satisfaction written all over her face. She had won this battle.

In a moment, peace had been restored on international sauce day, but we had also been given our first lesson. In a stand-off between my father and his sister-in-law, we had witnessed compromise.

My father loved his family, at times disputed, even his sister-in-law. And to those around him who were important enough to keep close to him, he would ultimately make allowances for.

I remembered once in a heated moment he had told my mother if she didn't like his ways then she should leave. I also remembered my mother climbing up onto a chair in their bedroom and took down an empty suitcase from the top of the cupboard. When she stepped down, she handed my father the suitcase and told him to go pack. She told him to put his belongings in there and get the hell out. She said that was the first and last time he would ever speak to her like that. From that moment on my father had learnt to compromise with her and to find a middle ground. My father knew he had a good thing and she wasn't going to be controlled or manipulated. I mean how boring would that be?

My mother was great at drama. She was a fantastic actor and extremely confident. My father, on the other hand wasn't.

The only balance of power he held in their relationship was where he sat each night to eat, at the head of the dining table.

My parents argued a lot, but to me that was just the norm. Conversations were loud in any Italian household. To get your point across you would have to be heard and I guess that meant turning up the volume dial. My parents respected one another, although at times I questioned it. I guess compromise comes easily when you have both invested in a relationship.

"Give and take," my mother would call this.

"I feed your father good food, give him his glass of vino with his meal and he's kept happy," she'd say.

"It's a much easier way to keep the peace, Emanuela. It doesn't require much sforzo (effort). Don't think too much about keeping them happy, it should come naturally," she'd say.

As I grew up, I began to understand what she meant. She had developed her own strategy and safe zone. She knew my father liked good food and she was a good cook. This was a happy middle ground for her. She had developed her own secret ingredient to getting what she wanted. After all, the way to a man's heart is through his stomach.

CHAPTER 5

ITALIANS DON'T EAT PRE-PACKAGED

ENATA'S FATHER PASSED away when she was only seven years old. She lived with her mother and older sister. Renata liked alternative. She only ate and smoked organic produce. We were raised to appreciate fresh, but she took it to the next level. We both had the same piercing green eyes and pale skin as our fathers did.

Rosie from my mother's side was more like my sister. Rosie was four years older and was at university, studying science. We all once worked together at a continental deli, but Rosie got to quit first. We hated it, but it allowed for a small income and an even smaller taste of independence.

Rosie was also the first to get her driver's licence and cruising around with her was fun, especially when we all got together.

"Rosie, can we please go for a drive? Ren wants to come too, please Rosie!" I asked one afternoon over the phone.

I had to whisper so my mother couldn't listen to my conversation. The phone was in the hallway and sometimes I stretched the cord to get it around the corner into the bathroom. If my mother caught me, she would slap me across the back of my head and take the phone from me. She would accuse me of breaking the phone. I wasn't allowed to use anything that was deemed too good at home in case I broke it. She said Italians didn't keep secrets from one another. I had to disclose all.

"Rosie, I want to meet boys, let's go driving, we can say we're going out for gelati," I said.

"I really want to go roller-skating at the new rink in town."

"Are you crazy, what if you hurt yourself? How would you explain that to your parents?" she asked.

"I really want to meet someone. Lots of boys go roller-skating. I hear the girls at school talking about the boys at the rink. I can't even meet a boy on the bus because I'm not even allowed to catch it!"

"I know Em, it's hard for us. It's not fair our parents are so strict. We're too scared to even kiss boys at this rate in case we get pregnant. I will never be this bad with my kids," Rosie said half joking.

I laughed. She was right. As if we'd even go there with boys, past first base.

"Rosie, we have to meet someone before we think about kids, what if we never do? What if we end up like Maria? The thought of ending up like her scares me. Why can't we go out, why is it that because we're girls we have to stay home?" I asked her.

"Is it wrong to want to have some fun?" I asked. "We're adults now."

"Em, you think too much and then you let it get the better of you. When the time is right, you'll meet someone. We all will. We can't predict these things," she said.

"Easy for you to say, you're at university and you get to socialise with the opposite sex, I'm at an all-girls school. I'm sick of helping my mum make fusilli just so Father Vincent can come over for lunch on Sundays. He's starting to look attractive to me. I'm tempted to play footsies with him under the table!" I said and we laughed.

"Emmie, you crack me up. I know it's tough now, but try to be optimistic, things can't be this bad forever. Times are changing," she said.

"I hope so, but I feel like even in this day and age I'm fighting for my freedom. Between bullshit cultural tradition and our parents' expectations, I'm stuck in a fucking time warp," I said.

"Yeah, I get that too, I don't even like Italian guys. I think I'll stay clear of them. I'm scared they'll have the same expectations as our parents. I'm not cooking for some wog boy. I don't want to pluck dead chickens just so they get to eat fresh. I don't want to cook and clean for them because they were raised on a pedestal. I want to be someone's wife, not their mother," she said.

"There's no equality when someone else is standing higher above you."

"Yeah, no kidding," I said.

"Okay let's go for a drive. Tell Renata we'll pick her up on the way."

Rosie had a bright yellow car. She refused to have the plastic red chilli pepper dangling from her rear vision mirror, supposedly to ward off evil. Instead she had chosen the fluffiest dice she could find, bright yellow with black dots, perfectly colour coordinated to match her car.

We liked driving with her because we stood out like a sore thumb, we wanted to be noticed. We all joked about it and said her car "glowed in the dark", it was hard to miss. We would drive around with the music up loud and the windows down. We would each buy the latest music cassettes to listen to in the car.

My cousins and I would have conversations about boys. We saw marriage as an avenue to gain freedom and independence. It made me sad to think that I had to look outside of my cultural heritage because I liked ethnic boys. I liked Greek boys the most. That was a no-go zone. There was no way on earth I would be able to date a Greek. In fact, I wasn't allowed to date at all, according to my father. I had to get married and skip the dating process altogether.

I wondered if back in my parent's day, they had arranged marriages. Where they would offer the boy's family a glory box filled with lavish sheet sets and embroidered towels in exchange for the girl's hand in marriage. *Oh God*, I thought to myself, I had a glory box sitting in my bedroom filled with white sheet sets.

It was so hard to get my head around the fact I was born in an entirely different country to my parents. A modern, beautiful country, and yet I felt pre-packaged. I wasn't allowed to be who I wanted to be. I wasn't allowed opinions on how I wanted my life to be. I wasn't allowed to express myself either. I wasn't allowed to explore options or use my own initiative to base my decisions on. These had already been decided for me. There was something inside of me that wanted to break free, but I wasn't even sure what that was. I was too busy filling my void with books and wanting to help others, I was letting myself down in the process.

Our cruising days with my cousins were my treat to help forget about all the "what-ifs" in my life.

"Rosie can you please drive me to see Pino?" I asked.

"He works at the continental deli in the western suburbs," I said.

"Yeah let's go to the west!" Renata said excitedly.

"Okay, let's do it! The west is uncharted territory. Let's do something bad for once," Rosie said.

We all lived in the eastern suburbs. The Italians who lived in the west side of the city were different and the boys had an edge to them. They weren't as refined as the eastern boys.

They were known as the bad boys. We weren't allowed to date boys from the west or the north of the city. We had to stick with the suburbs our parents thought were the most civilized and best suited for us. The northerners were market gardeners and they were looked down upon. The west side Italians were crazy, according to our parents, and weren't "real" Italians. My father said they spoke an entirely different language although it was still Italian.

Renata put her tape in the cassette player of the car, she turned up the volume. We were listening to Pat Benatar singing *'All Fired Up'*. The windows were down and the breeze brushing my fringe away from my face.

"I'm really interested in Pino. His cousin, Pina goes to my school and he came to pick her up a few times last week. I got to chat with him by the front school gate and I asked his cousin for his number. I called him the other day. I was so nervous! But he said if I'm ever around the west side to go see him and say hello," I explained, as Rosie drove.

"Hasn't she got more than one cousin called Pino? I thought there were five of them. Are you sure you got the right one?" Renata said.

"Of course, I've got the right one! He's so cute and he seemed nice enough. He asked me about school and what I got up to on the weekends. He's only my height though," I said.

"Why are Italian guys so short?" Renata asked.

"According to my mother, they weren't fed oranges as kids and missed out on vitamins," Rosie joked.

We arrived at the deli. I could see the legs of prosciutto hanging and the wheels of cheese from the front window. I quickly applied my fuchsia lipstick and puffed up my hair with my hands.

I leant over to my cousins from the back seat, "I'm so nervous!" I said.

"We didn't drive all this way for you to back down now, GO!" Rosie instructed.

"Okay, okay!" I replied, and I got out of the car.

I walked towards the front door of the deli. I turned back and saw Rosie and Renata moving their hands ushering me to go in. We didn't have much time. We had to get back home.

As I walked in, I saw Pino behind the counter. It was higher than the shop floor. He stood taller than me. I should have taken that as a sign. There was no one else in the shop.

"Hi, Pino!" I said nervously.

Pino tilted his head to one side, he had a white t-shirt on, and his hair was slicked back with gel. I saw a thick gold chain with a giant cross hanging around his neck glistening in the light.

"It's me, Emmie," I said, beginning to feel anxious.

"Remember? We spoke at school when you came to pick your cousin up," I added.

"Oh yeah, you're the chick who rang me yeah?"

"Yes," I replied.

We began to chat. After ten minutes I had become conscious of the time and the nervous perspiration building up under my armpits.

"Pino would you like to meet for gelati sometime?" I quickly blurted out, my fear kicking my confidence into play.

"Um Emmie, I don't think so. You're still in high school and I don't do gelati. I do Saturday night discos with my mates. Pina should mind her own business because I don't date girls from the east side. Don't take it personally, but you're too young and not my type. We're from different backgrounds," he said.

I stiffened and felt my face heating up.

With his rejection replaying in my mind, I felt as if he had slapped me across the head with a leg of prosciutto hanging behind him. In fact, I wished he had, to wake me up from this humiliating nightmare.

"Oh, okay. That's cool, Pino. It was only a suggestion. I'd better go. My cousins are waiting for me," I said as I turned to walk to the door.

I could feel my face starting to burn and sting, like the time I fell asleep sunbathing and woke to a red-hot beetroot face.

When I sat back in the car both my cousins were waiting in anticipation.

"What did he say?" they both asked.

"He said not to take it personally, but he doesn't date eastern girls," I said sounding disappointed.

"Apparently we are from different backgrounds," I said.

"What the fuck does that mean?" Renata asked.

She was right, what did it mean exactly?

"Different backgrounds! We're not talking about sopressa salami and mettwurst. We're talking about sopressa salami and capocollo, it's still Italian salami. Whichever way you look at it you still shove it into your panino and eat it! It's just a different cut," Renata went on to say.

We began to laugh.

"Well I guess when you put it that way Ren, you've got a point," I said.

Don't take it personally, I thought. Well, actually, I did take disappointment personally. I had feelings. Maybe my expectations were a little high, but with my limited options I guess I was hoping and wishing a little too hard. Of course, I was going to take it personally, I felt humiliated and I felt like a fool. I wanted to meet him for gelati and build my confidence up around boys. I wasn't going to propose to the guy. I wanted a new friend not a husband.

Driving back home we were all a little quiet. Renata had the music turned down.

"Hey, I know this nice guy for you!" Rosie piped up.

"I went to school with him, his name is Dave Smith," she said.

Dave Smith, I thought to myself, funnily enough I'd always liked the surname 'Smith' as a kid. It suited the Australian culture well. It didn't sound pre-packaged.

CHAPTER 6

POINT-BLANK

My father was finally going to teach me how to drive. I had my learners permit and he had decided it was time. He no longer had the time to drive my mother around. He was passing that role over to me. He was time poor and found it hard scheduling in my mother so she could do her grocery shopping or banking. He was good at giving instructions and thought it shouldn't take me long to get behind the wheel of a car.

My father was busy working and building homes for others. My mother and I spent a lot of time at home together. When he wasn't home, he was taking trips overseas back to Italy to visit his mother. He would spend many months there when he could.

Rosie's mother, my mother's younger sister, drove. I couldn't believe the difference in progression they both had in their thinking and their lives. My mother was older and so were her traditions that she brought over to Australia. Apparently, her trip to Australia took three months by ship. When her sister was old enough to join her, she flew over and so did her modern ideas. My mother was set in her ways. Rosie liked to refer to my mother as 'antique'.

Rosie's mother got her driver's licence when she was in her early fifties. She had enough of catching public transport everywhere. She hired an Italian driving instructor and in no time was on the road to freedom. My father encouraged my mother to get hers as well, but she chose not to and was now regretting it. My mother was so confident, strong and resilient in her life, however the one time she doubted herself she lost her chance to learn how to drive and her chance for greater independence. She used to ride a motorcycle in her early 20's, so fear certainly wasn't a contributing factor. I think she secretly liked being driven around by my father.

It was a real pain when my father was away overseas, my mother and I had to catch the bus to go buy groceries, lugging it back home was backbreaking. We'd have bottles of Chinotto clinking away loudly and God help us when she bought a kilo of pecorino cheese. An entire bus full of people could smell it. They would all stare at us like we were some foreigners with weird stinky food. I loved my Italian cheese and Italian cola. They could stare all they liked, I didn't care. They probably didn't know how good it tasted anyway. I didn't like the plastic variety of cheese they ate. And un-wrapping it was annoying. It didn't taste real and the plastic annoyingly stuck to the cheese. It tasted awful, especially when I'd forget to unwrap it and accidentally grill it on my bread.

My father always had nice cars. I couldn't wait to get my full licence and drive. Sometimes I would sneak into the garage and just sit in his car and smell the leather interior. He kept it so clean and shiny. Even the carpets smelt freshly shampooed. My father would wash his car each weekend. He was car proud just as my mother was house proud.

I would work at a continental deli on weekends and some days after school. I was hoping to save enough money to buy my own car. I wanted my independence too.

"Emanuela, put the learner's sticker on the car," my father instructed me.

I had purchased magnet learner stickers so he could start taking me out for driving lessons. He insisted he was a better teacher than my instructor who would limit my learning to shopping centre carparks.

"I am going to take you on the main road. You need to learn with real cars around," he said.

I liked my instructor. He was a nice, elderly Italian man called Alfredo who taught my aunt how to drive. He was calm, he wouldn't yell at me. I had my reservations about my father teaching me how to drive, I was scared. I didn't want him yelling at me, and I didn't feel ready driving on the main road either. Alfredo always had a box of tissues handy that he kept in the car, when I would become anxious my hands would perspire. He was so thoughtful and said there was no rush getting me out onto a main road. My father disagreed and thought Alfredo was ripping him off. He said it shouldn't be taking me this long to get out on the road.

I got into his car and put my seatbelt on. I turned on the ignition. The sheepskin seat cover felt soft and cosy.

"Emanuela, check your mirrors before you start reversing out of the driveway!" he said.

I was already starting to perspire, and my hands began to feel slippery across the leather steering wheel. My father didn't keep tissues in his car. Instead he had a red chilli pepper hanging from his rear vision mirror that was dangling like a carrot to a rabbit. It was distracting to watch it sway from side to side.

I was listening intently not to miss any part of his instructions. My lesson started well, sticking to the back streets. Once we had driven around a while we ended up back on the main road where he told me to turn right onto a major highway. My perspiration went into overdrive. Like God parting the Red Sea, I had sweat dripping on both sides of my face. I thought I was going to drown like the Egyptian army once Moses closed the parting sea. I didn't feel safe driving in the middle lane of a three-lane highway.

My father began to sense my fear.

"Stick to the speed limit, you are going too slow Emanuela," he said.

"Follow the white line on the road," he instructed.

There were cars passing us and beeping, even though they could see I was a learner driver. I didn't feel safe driving in the middle of the road. I wanted to be in the left lane close to the curb in case I had to pull over. I had cars zooming past me on both sides. His way of teaching me to overcoming my fears was facing them head on. The only thing I feared facing head on were the massive semi-trailer trucks passing us on the opposite side of the highway.

"Emanuela, if you stick to the speed limit and you watch the cars in front of you, and you do the right thing you have nothing to worry about," he said.

Do the right thing, I thought to myself, I have to do the right thing?

What if I wanted to turn around and go home, was that wrong? What if I wasn't ready to face my fears just yet? How significant were my fears at sixteen anyway? They were bloody significant at that point in time out in the middle of a major highway.

I increased the speed of the car and I planted my foot down on the accelerator. I was annoyed and tired, and as I did, a big truck passed us on the right-hand side. I could feel its wind force. It felt like I was driving in a wind tunnel. With all that force besides me, the front learner driver magnet flew straight across the top of the car. In an instant, my natural instincts kicked in and I turned my head to look back and see it flying away down the road. My father went crazy. He was swearing in Italian. I had never seen him go so nuts. He completely lost it. He was screaming at me to look at the car in front and to never turn around to look at the cars at the back. He was yelling at me to keep my eyes on the road in front.

"There's nothing to see back there. If you are travelling straight ahead that's where your focus should lie. Not somewhere back there!" he screeched.

"Doing what you just did could get us killed or injured!"

In one driving lesson my father had taught me how to face my fears. His yelling no longer influenced me, mainly because I had lost partial hearing in my left ear from his screaming.

He taught me that I had nothing to fear if I remained focused and followed the rules. He also taught me to not look back, keep moving forward. There are only certain times that looking back is called for and they weren't that often.

I was no longer perspiring. In fact, I was trying not to laugh, because I think I had instilled fear in my father. He said I could keep my driving lessons with my instructor, he was happy to keep paying for them.

I couldn't wait to get home to ring Rosie and tell her. I had killed two birds with one stone. I had faced my fears and made my father perspire in the process. He had little beads of sweat dripping from his forehead. He pulled out his monogrammed handkerchief and wiped them away.

I began to think about the crush I once had on Pino and how he told me not to take things personally. I realised my father's driving lesson was more than just how to drive. He taught me if I looked straight ahead whatever happened in the past was a lot easier to let go of. If I was focused on going forward whatever happened back down the highway no longer mattered, we had already driven past it.

CHAPTER 7

BLOODY NORA

Y COUSINS AND I were a dynamic working party. Problem solving growing up had to be inventive. Meeting boys were high on our agenda. I mean, isn't that what most teenagers want to do? Meet someone and dabble in relationships where we can experience the 'first kiss'. Most of my experiences with boys came straight out of the books I read. My favourite book growing up was *Superfudge* by Judy Blume, but now I preferred reading *Forever* by her instead.

Getting around what we wanted from our parents was tricky and it involved forward planning. If we were ever caught doing the wrong thing, our parents would go mental, no matter how old we were. We had to live by their rules, not those governed by Australian laws.

Rosie had discovered Green Grasshopper cocktails. She tried them at a university bar and had become so addicted to the creamy alcohol she insisted we tried them too. She enlisted the help of me and Renata to get her to a bar one Saturday night.

Christmas was looming and our parents were busy so we had to seize the opportunity.

We weren't allowed to go out on a Saturday night with friends. Saturday nights were spent visiting other relatives with our parents, boring when you're in your late teens. Sitting around listening to meaningless conversations, not allowed to take anything to eat from the table offered to you either. You weren't allowed to be perceived as rude or hungry by others. Aimlessly salivating at chocolate wagon wheels put out by the host was a normal Saturday night. When temptation got the better of me, I'd get the secret pinch under the table from my mother or the death stare from my father.

If my cousins and I were going to achieve an outcome, it had to be like a synchronized swimming routine worthy of gold. We had to work together.

"Rosie," I whispered down the phone line.

I was looking out for my mother.

"Have you thought of a plan yet?" I heard Rosie whisper back.

"Yes, I have. I ran it past Renata today at the deli," I said.

"I have every faith in you Em. I'm really excited. I met this guy at university a while ago and he wants to join us, I just have to call him with the details. We have to go to this new bar, it used to be an old tunnel that has been turned into a disco," she said.

"Yeah, I've heard of it from some of the girls at school. So, the plan is to say that we're all going to midnight mass together. Our mums and Maria are going to be tired from all the cooking and baking and won't fully register what I tell them. I'm going to say that we're going to meet them at church at midnight. Fingers crossed, they'll be too tired to go so that might buy us more time," I suggested.

"They'll want our help cooking and baking," Rosie said.

"I'll tell them that Father Vincent has asked for our help setting up the church for the mass. I'll go see him straight from work. I'll bring him a panino as a good-will gesture. Then I'll go to Ren's house and change. Her mum and Maria will already be at my place as will yours. You can pick us up from Ren's," I suggested.

"Em, I love it. That will give us plenty of time. I'll come by the deli tomorrow when Ren is there and we can fine tune our plan. How do you come up with this sort of stuff?" she asked.

"It's taking a risk. It should all work according to the plan if we stick to it. We have to keep an eye on Renata, she might go wondering off though," I said.

Christmas time growing up was special. My mother would decorate the house with fancy ornaments and we would put the Christmas tree up together. She would choose the prettiest angel for the top. She had the same Italian linen Christmas tablecloth she would use each year with matching table wear. The boxes of panettone would be lined up in the good room that no one could touch or eat. Nothing was too hard for her when it came to cooking for the festivities. The food was always delicious.

My father would save his best soppressata (dry salami) and prosciutto to cut up and we would eat chunks with provolone cheese and the freshest continental bread.

My cousins and I were always plotting and planning something. Our plans would include smoking a cigarette or skolling a few shots of grappa without being caught. I guess that's where we developed our need for excitement, doing something bad and getting away with it.

When I arrived home from work, I went outside to greet my aunts and cousin. As soon as I walked into the outside kitchen, I could smell the pasta flour. I saw the big white bag spread out on the wooden table and cartons of fresh eggs.

I greeted everyone, kissing them all on the cheek.

"Ma, I'm going to help Father Vincent after work to set up the church for midnight mass," I said.

My mother, older cousin Maria and my aunts were rolling out sheets of pasta for the lasagna. All four of them had their aprons on. They were working together.

One was turning the pasta machine handle, the other feeding dough into it.

"What a good girl you are Emanuela, look at my Emanuela," my mother flaunted.

"Always helping at church," she said.

"You got a boyfriend yet, Emanuela?" Rosie's mother asked.

I saw Maria roll her eyes. They had all but given up on her ever finding someone, preferring to pin their hopes on the younger generation. Maria had been unlucky in love.

"No zia I'm too busy studying," I said.

"Va bene, bella," she replied as she went back to kneading more pasta dough.

I wasn't going to fall for one of their trick questions. Even if I did have a boyfriend it would be a well-kept secret. I'd never tell any of them anything.

"Get off her back, she's still young," Maria piped up.

"Are you all going to mass tonight?" I asked, phishing for clues.

"We haven't decided yet, we might be too tired. We still have a lot of cooking and preparation to do," Maria said.

"Maria can you please make crostoli since you have the pasta maker out?" I asked.

"You know how much we all love your recipe. Christmas wouldn't be the same without them," I added.

"Yes, si, si we must make them too!" my mother exclaimed.

Now I was sure they'd be too tired for midnight mass. I had securely planted the seed for more baking.

Maria looked at me, horrified. If looks could kill, I would have been dead on the spot. She looked so old and tired. She had white flour lightly dusted on her face from the kneading she had done. She was a large, plump woman with a round face. She had a dark mole on her left cheek with a pesky hair sticking out.

She was the driving force behind turning the pasta machine by hand. The rest of the women were a lot older and complained of arthritis. I felt sorry for Maria. This was her life now. Taking care of the older generation, it was seen as her duty. There was no hope for her future. She was too old to ever have children. She missed the boat. She was once left at the altar and never overcame her broken heart. She accepted her life as it was.

She wiped the flour away from her face with the back of her hand, "Yes Emmie, I'll make crostoli," Maria complied.

"Okay ma, I'm going to work now. Ciao tutti (all)," I said.

I grabbed my bag and set off. It contained all the necessities for a night out. Fuchsia pink lipstick, plum-coloured eyeshadows and floral perfume. My own kit. The excitement was running through my veins like the morning cocktail my mother would make me drink for 'strength' before school. Only this time I wasn't going to be drinking marsala and warm milk. I was looking forward to a few Green Grasshoppers myself.

The day flew by as it does when you actually have something to look forward to. I made certain that Renata was completely coherent and up to scratch in her part of the plan.

After I had dropped off Father Vincent's food, we made our way to Renata's house to get ready.

Renata's bedroom quickly filled up with a misty haze of hairspray and clothes scattered on her bed.

"Renata, can you please do my makeup?" I asked, handing her my kit.

"You have a real knack at this sort of thing and I like your black eyeliner," I said.

"Sure, I'd love to," she replied.

"Let's have a drink," she suggested.

She left her bedroom and returned to hold a bottle with orange coloured liquid in it and two glasses.

"I've got this mandarin liqueur my mum made," Renata said, pouring some in the shot glasses. The aroma was intoxicating as it hit the tiny glasses. It smelt citrusy and sweet.

"Ren, that's the best stuff I've ever tried!" I said, taking a sip.

It was easy to drink, smooth and sweet.

We heard Rosie pull up at the front of the house and ran to open the door.

"Rosie, how did you get your hair so puffy?" I asked.

"There's this new hair product called mousse," she said.

"Wow."

Renata and I both went up to her, looking and feeling her hair. It smelt like a vanilla milkshake. It was all puffy and permed, but held its shape perfectly minus the sticky lacquer.

"Are you girls ready? I can't wait to have a few drinks. We finally managed to get a free pass out, how awesome is this!" Rosie said.

"Yeah, but we have to go to midnight mass, we have to stick together no matter what. We have to be there on time," I said, reminding them both our freedom came at a price and curfew.

"Please Renata don't go wondering off or doing anything stupid tonight," I said.

"I promise I won't!" she replied.

When we arrived, the club was packed with people. I felt my head was spinning because we were so far underground. It felt like there wasn't enough oxygen to go around in the tiny cramped tunnel. My mind went into overdrive thinking what a bad idea this was and all the 'what-ifs' associated with our night out in a disco. It was a sin to lie and we did just that, on a grand scale. I was the leader of the pack, the instigator, and the brains behind this.

I thought of the wooden Pinocchio doll Rosie had in her bedroom, a reminder not to lie to our parents. We already had well-defined noses. I began to feel claustrophobic standing in a tunnel packed with people brushing up against me. Rosie could sense I was beginning to feel the pressure and handed me a green drink.

I took one sip. "Oh this tastes so good Rosie!" I said, quickly sipping more through my tiny paper straw.

"I know right," she said.

Rosie wandered off to her friends nearby. I kept an eye on Renata talking to boys. I was standing at the bar when a man came tumbling towards me. He was wearing a red and black-checkered flannel shirt and jeans and had sandy blonde hair.

"Bloody Nora, I've stubbed me toe!" he said, leaning on me to balance while he grabbed his foot.

"What?" I asked, trying to shake his arm off of me.

"My toe, I got it caught in a bar stood," he said.

"I didn't see it, there's no light in this place."

He stood up straight. I looked down at his worn tan boots with his right boot sporting a black mark from the bar stool he spoke of.

"I'm Dean by the way. I'm down for the weekend from the mid-north for the Country Christmas Show," he went on to say.

"Hi, I'm Emmie," I said, sounding disappointed.

Why did I attract this guy? I mean, Dean was as Aussie as I was ever going to get. I liked the Greek looking guy I was eyeing off at the end of the bar who had the same hairdo as Rosie. Why couldn't *he* come and talk to me? I had made eye contact with him from the moment we walked down the stairs.

The music was loud and the DJ had begun to play *'Freedom'* by Wham! I turned to look at the Greek boy who had hit the dance floor with his friends. He had a black shirt on and a white jacket and blue jeans. He was a good dancer, then he turned and looked at me. He had a sexy smile. Like a bad boy.

I could barely hear Dean speaking over the music.

"Wanna beer, Emmie?" Dean asked.

"What?" I asked.

He pointed to his glass of beer.

I smiled, "Sure Dean, I'll have a beer."

"You look like a decent sheila," he said with a smile.

I was scanning the room for Renata, when she walked in my direction. I grabbed her by the arm and pulled her in towards me. She looked at Dean with a big grin on her face. She liked Aussie boys, it was her way of rebelling against her upbringing.

"Dean, this is my cousin Renata," I said introducing them.

Renata looked at Dean, her eyes locking with his and her face lighting up.

We were chatting with cold beers in hand. Rosie was off with her university friends. Renata and Dean hit it off and I began to feel like the third wheel. I left them to talk and I wandered around the club. I caught the Greek's attention and walked over to him.

Our girl's night out went according to plan. No sooner had we arrived it was time to leave. Driving back to church seemed fitting. I felt like I had to ask God for forgiveness for lying to my parents and kissing a Greek boy with fluffy hair.

I could still smell Con's aftershave on my top. I managed to talk to him after all and he was a good kisser. My father was wrong, Greek boys didn't taste like lamb.

"Em, you're the best. You executed this plan perfectly. I really like Dean! He gave me his number and he seemed so genuine. I love Aussie guys, they're what you see is what you get. You don't get those sorts of guys coming into the deli. I had the best time," Renata said.

"I'm glad you had fun, Ren. It was a team effort. Dean seems like a really nice guy," I said.

"I barely understood him. I thought Bloody Nora was a cocktail, but instead he bought me a beer," I said.

"No silly, that's a Bloody Mary!" they laughed.

I sat in the back seat of the car feeling pleased with myself. I looked into my compact mirror to tidy up my makeup. I saw the skin of my face turn a slight shade of green. I was beginning to feel sick.

We drove up the windy driveway to the church and parked by the nativity. When we got out of the car, I could hear the Christmas hymns played over the loudspeaker. I spotted my father amongst the crowd now gathering for midnight mass. He was looking around trying to spot us. There were children playing on the front lawn of the church screeching in delight at the thought of Santa arriving.

The night was warm and the heat hit my face. My Grasshoppers began to make their way up and out. The cream had churned in my stomach with the beer.

"Em, are you okay?" Rosie asked after noticing me leaning up against her car. I was going to vomit but I didn't want my father spotting me.

"I will be in a minute," I said, quickly departed.

I headed towards the large nativity by the side of the church. I could smell the fresh bales of hay inside of it. I walked behind it, pulled back my long hair and vomited on a small patch of grass.

"Em, bloody hell," I heard Renata laughing behind me.

I stood up, "All good girls, let's go to church," I said.

"Lesson to be learnt, don't mix your drinks," I turned to them and said.

CHAPTER 8

Rosie was secretly planning on moving interstate. She had been applying for jobs and I was devastated at the thought of losing her. She had Melbourne set in her sights. She didn't run her plan past her parents. She wanted to move as far away as possible.

She had finally finished her genetic science degree, her first taste of freedom. She was a university graduate. Her parents were throwing her a big graduation party, at a small community hall, with a sit-down dinner reminiscent of an Italian wedding.

My mother and father had purchased a tan coloured leather-bound brief case with her initials monogrammed on the top as a gift. Not many Italian women graduated from university in the '80s. Most of us were expected to marry and have children and careers weren't really factored into our lives. We had part-time work that gave us an allowance, and our parents provided the rest, a roof over our heads and food to eat. It was perceived our future husbands would then take over.

I didn't want to get married to remain at home and have children. How was I even going to meet someone anyway? I wasn't allowed to go out and now that Rosie was leaving, it would be so much harder. At least with her around we could sneak in a drive or two.

I was not dealing well with the news. Although Rosie and I made plans to write to one another, it just wasn't going to be the same.

"We can tape conversations on our cassette player, and post them to one another," Rosie suggested.

"Yeah, I guess so. My parents won't let me call you every night. They don't like me using the phone as it is. They probably see it as my lifeline to the outside world."

"We can write to one another too. The post-box is just down the road from you," Rosie said.

"It won't be the same without you. I'll miss our drives, I'll miss you so much," I said.

"Same," Rosie said. "It won't be easy for me either. I'll have to make new friends. I'll have to find a place to live. My mum will do my head in, insisting she has a say in everything I do."

"My parents are already on my back about getting married now that I'm about to turn eighteen. How am I supposed to meet anyone? I can't go out. They're all old at church. No one goes to the 8 o'clock Italian mass on a Sunday morning. All the cute guys go to the 10 o'clock English mass," I said.

"Now that you've decided that you're leaving, I'll have nothing to look forward to," I said.

Rosie was a lot more mature than I was, and she was more like an older sister to me. Renata on the other hand was not. Renata was different. She had issues with her upbringing. We all did, but Renata preferred the self-medicating method of coping. Refusing to find strategies outside of her intoxicated, fume infested, poster covered bedroom walls.

I was finishing up my final year of high school and I found it hard. I fit in at an all-girls Catholic school, and I liked learning. In fact, secretly I wanted to go to university too, but I didn't have a ding-a-ling between my legs. I was struggling with fighting for change, fighting for acceptance and fighting for freedom in my own birthplace. Shouldn't my citizenship give me exempt rights to live in a democratic society? Yes, it should. But my cultural upbringing would not allow it.

I was blessed to at least have my cousins in my life.

Renata lived down the road from me. We would have some of our best conversations in her bedroom. When she remained focused.

"Renata I'm upset about Rosie leaving us soon. I feel like she's already had a job offer and she hasn't told us. I've noticed a change in her, she's been really happy lately. For me, her moving away feels life changing. My parents won't let me visit her in a different state. I'll only get to see her if she comes back home. I'm happy for her, I truly am. I'm happy she's found her freedom. But I feel like I'm still four years behind her before it's my turn."

"I'm sad too, but she hasn't even left yet. We still have time with her. We can have fun together if you get your head out of the stupid books you read. You can't change and grow if you lock yourself away in your bedroom. Loss forces growth."

I looked at Renata with total surprise on my face. My eyes wide open. I began to feel anger. Renata was lecturing me when she was still stuck in disappointment herself, locked in her bedroom, away from the world.

Renata had dropped out of school. She didn't have the same desire to learn as I did and she preferred to listen to music rather than read. She preferred to think of herself as a free spirit and not tied down to anything. I liked structure in my life. I liked to forward plan.

"I don't want to go to her graduation dinner. I don't think I'll cope with my sister trying to set me up with some loser when she can't find someone for herself. I'm going to need some help," she said, as she pulled out her glass toy.

"Ren, seriously, do you have to smoke that now? I don't want to go to this party smelling like marijuana. I've just had my hair done! I know the pressure is on us to meet someone, but find other ways to deal with it. I'll see you tonight at Rosie's party. I'm going home!" I said, irritated, leaving abruptly.

I was annoyed at times with Renata and the way she coped with things. She was preaching to me about growth when she was still stuck within her own grief. We all had to accept her behaviour because her father passed away when she was only seven years old. She experienced loss at a young age and had never moved beyond that. We were all expected to accept her and her poor choices. She seemed to lack common sense and maturity. She was challenging at times to be around.

Rosie and I would have intelligent conversations how we could support one another when life got tough. We would find solutions on how to cope with our stifled upbringing. She was lucky and she met boys at her school. I never did. She was allowed to attend a unisex school. It was diagonally across the road from where she lived. If it was convenient for our parents and it suited their needs at the time, then it was okay, otherwise we were mostly seen as an inconvenience.

The most rebellious thing Rosie and I ever did was smoke the occasional cigarette and swear when out of earshot of the adults. Renata didn't like the tobacco type. She had decided to grow her own variety amongst her mother's vegetable patch. Her mother had found her dried supply in the back shed once and thought it was oregano and had sprinkled some in her pasta sauce. We all felt very unwell that night after dinner. Stupid Renata nearly killed us all.

I never understood how she could get away with such things and I couldn't. I was the 'good' girl in the family and expectations were placed high on me. I was the one who followed the rules, and didn't break them.

I was glad I still had some time left with Rosie and I was looking forward to her party. Maybe I would meet someone there?

All the guests were lined up waiting to talk to Rosie and her parents. She was dressed in a cream coloured suit, her hair permed and curly, heavily lacquered to stay in place. I was wearing a new dress, teal green with an open back and large shoulder pads. I had matching teal green drop earrings and white high heel shoes.

Once inside, we took our seats at the round dinner tables where antipasto and warm crusty oil bread rolls were waiting. They smelt even more delicious knowing I couldn't eat it in fear of the crumbs sticking to my fuchsia pink lipstick.

I scanned the room to see if anyone caught my eye. I could see Rosie's university friends sitting down one end of the hall and her family members at the other end. I was looking forward to meeting some of them. I was trying hard to ignore Renata sitting next to me high as a kite and laughing like a lunatic.

Once the formalities were over, the DJ began playing '80s music and phased out the Italian wedding songs. '*The Chicken Dance*' and the '*La Tarantella*' were enjoyed by our mothers, returning to their seats puffed out and fanning themselves with paper napkins. He began to play Bon Jovi and the younger crowd began to mingle with the older men going outside to smoke. The guests seemed to relax.

Rosie came over and grabbed me by my hand to introduce me to some of her friends.

"Emmie this is Bernie and his girlfriend Anna," Rosie said, working her way around the tables.

"Pleased to meet you," I said.

"And this is my old school friend, Dave," she said.

"Hello, Dave," I said.

"Hi Emmie," he said happily.

"Rosie mentioned you work at the deli across the road from the church."

"Yes, I do. I work there after school some days," I replied.

"I might come in one day. I don't live far from there," he said.

"Sure," I said flippantly.

I don't know why he'd want to come into the deli, I thought to myself. What would he buy?

Dave Smith seemed like any other Aussie guy. He seemed decent enough, but I wasn't really interested in him. He didn't seem my type. I didn't have any butterflies in my stomach like I did with Pino. I didn't have sweaty palms and I certainly didn't have skipped heart beats. Instead, I had an annoying frown trying to hear him speak, because he was so meek and quiet. I couldn't even gauge the emotion as his hands were neatly placed in his lap and not waving about. He was nicely dressed, but too nerdy for me. Someone you'd find volunteering his lunchtimes going through the lost and found box and recording all of the items at school. He looked like someone who kept to himself and wouldn't be able to handle an Italian challenge. Too well organised for me. He didn't seem like a risk taker and I wanted someone with an edge to them. I wanted someone who would make my big green eyes even bigger each time they walked into a room. Someone, who would take my breath away. Dave didn't seem to possess any of these qualities and I wasn't going to waste my time or his.

"Dave is such a nice guy Em, what do you think?" Rosie asked me.

"Forget it!" I said.

CHAPTER 9

DECENCY IS WAY HOTTER

Dave BECAME A regular at the deli. He would visit most days I was there. He would come in to buy Swiss cheese and continental bread. I was surprised at the reoccurring purchase as he looked like he was choking whenever he ate it. I felt like I should have a glass of water on standby just in case.

I would cut him a piece of cheese each time, like the butcher would slice me a piece of fritz as a child. In the same motion I would diligently hand him a piece over the counter once I had removed the wax. He'd politely accept it and looked like a happy little mouse nibbling away. He took his time eating, unlike Italians. We ate fast preferring to scoff our food, briefly coming up for air.

Funnily enough when I explained this to Dave, he was surprised I had never experienced heartburn or indigestion. I explained it was only the Asian variety that I had food sensitivities to. He showed a real appreciation for our food.

I wasn't keen on Dave, but I was polite to him, most of the time. I loved Rosie and I realised she only had my best interest at heart, but I wished she had never introduced me to Dave. I couldn't get rid of the guy. He was quiet and shy, or so he seemed to be. It was when he began to look at me differently that worried me. He would star-gaze. I wasn't interested in him, he was someone who hung around waiting for my attention. At times I would throw him scraps here and there because I felt sorry for him.

"Hello Emmie! Have you been busy today?" Dave asked excitedly.

"Hi Dave, yes I have," I fibbed. "I haven't got much time to talk today."

The deli had been quiet for most of the day. I didn't want Dave hanging around, I wasn't in the mood. I wanted to get rid of him as soon as possible. I had to be smart and not let him push my buttons because each time I did, he seemed to enjoy it and smiled. That would infuriate me even more.

He stood by the counter watching me wiping down the benches.

"Emmie, Rosie said that your dad leaves for Italy soon. Do you think your mum would let you go out to dinner with me? I want to take you to my favourite Italian restaurant. They make the best tortellini all panna," he asked.

"I don't think so, Dave. Plus, she makes the best pasta, so I guess the answer to your question is no," I said trying to put him off.

Asking an Italian to an Italian restaurant was the dumbest suggestion. *I bet he eats his pizza with pineapple on it too,* I thought, eyeing him up and down. He really stirred something up in me and it wasn't butterflies. It was more like a swarm of bees.

"What if I asked her?" he suggested.

"Are you out of your mind!" I snapped, nearly hitting my head on fridge door taking out a wheel of Swiss cheese. "You can't just ask my mum if I can go out with you!"

"Why not? It's not an unreasonable ask."

"Because things don't operate like that Dave, in an Italian household we have rules! I can't just leave the house when I want to," I explained.

"But you're an adult and I want to have dinner with you. Rosie is visiting from Melbourne, maybe your mum will let you go with her and I can meet you both later?" he suggested.

I handed him a slice of cheese, "I'll have a think about it," I said.

"Thanks for the cheese, Emmie. I know you care about me," he said with a wink and a smile, then turning to leave.

Smartarse.

Rosie had moved and I had assimilated to life without her. This was something I had no choice but to accept. I had to make do with Renata in small doses. I missed Rosie so much. I missed our conversations over the occasional cigarette, feeling like 'bad' girls whenever we would sneak one in.

"Rosie, Dave came in to see me again at work today. I can't get rid of the guy," I said when I called her later that evening.

"Have you been out to dinner with him yet? He said he was going to ask you," she phished.

"Yes, he asked me, he even sent me flowers. I want someone who's hot. I want someone exciting, someone who has an edge, not a nerdy accountant. He talks to me about bank accounts and budgeting. He tells me how he helps people profit from the work they do. He talks like he's a finance guru. He's kind of boring. He's not a blokey-bloke and he eats tortellini alla panna. That's not even a real sauce!" I said. We both laughed.

"He's a decent guy Em. He's good looking and he likes you a lot. He's trying to include you in his life. I think the hot guys and bad boys out there are trouble. I swear they break girls' hearts because they know they can. I think those sorts of guys would have very little respect for girls and very high expectations," she said.

"Not necessarily, not if they love you," I replied.

"There's so much more to loving someone than just the feeling of butterflies in your stomach or saying the word itself. Love is a commitment and it seems Dave is very committed to getting your attention. It's the way we're treated as well. Love involves respect and reassurance that they'll stick around no matter what. It's everlasting. Love should bring happiness not heartache. It's the effort they put in. Real love takes time to evolve, an opportunity to genuinely get to know one another. Em, the guy sent you flowers, he's trying. Look at him as a friend first. Like him, instead of looking at loving him."

"I hadn't looked at it in that way."

"You're right, he is putting in a huge effort. I don't dislike him. I'll think about going out to dinner with him. I should give the guy a break, I guess. We'll see," I said.

"Em, I went out on a date the other night."

"What, with who!" I prodded.

"This guy from work. He's cute, we've been meeting up for coffees during our lunch breaks. His name is Karl, he works as a junior radiologist. But we're only friends at the moment. I want to establish myself within my career first. I do like him, but there's no future with him, he's German," she said.

I began to laugh.

"Your mum won't approve! That's as bad as me dating a Greek guy!"

"Have you guys kissed?" I asked.

"Yeah, he's a great kisser. But something happened the other night and I'm really worried because my mum and dad are visiting next week!"

"What?" I asked. Surely, she didn't sleep with him?

"Well, he gave me a love bite."

"Oh, okay. So, wear a scarf," I suggested.

"On my nose!" she said.

"What! how?" I laughed. "Is that even possible?"

"Yes, it sure is! He sucked my nose right off. He began kissing my neck and slowly making his way across kissing my face. Then he began to slowly suck my nose, he sucked on it like sucking a frozen Snip," she said.

"He wouldn't stop. He took a little nibble at first, then it felt like a little bite, but we were caught up in the throes of things. It was pretty heated. He just kept sucking away. When he stopped, he had this look of horror on his face and began apologising. It wasn't until the next day I noticed my nose was really red and bruised. I can't stand my nose. It sticks out so far, but Karl loves it, he says it's bony. I was too embarrassed to say anything to him at the time, he's the first guy I've ever really done anything with. At first, I thought nose sucking was normal, but now looking at it, clearly it's not. I actually have teeth marks on my nose!"

"Rosie, I'm lost for words. You better wear some makeup. Your mum will spot those teeth marks from a mile away! You're dealing with the Italian FBI. If she spots any evidence of a love bite, you'll have her scraping his DNA off your face! I teased.

"It could only happen to you!" I laughed.

"I feel so inexperienced, but Karl is so patient. I'll just have to tell my mother I walked into a door or something."

Shortly after my phone conversation, I began to think about what love looked like to me. I thought about what Rosie had said and she was right, love was a commitment and began with strong friendship. I was raised with morals and values so it was hard to grasp there were people in the world who would intentionally hurt others. I viewed love as a team effort, both people investing in a relationship.

I thought about my parents. Although they were loud, they accepted each other. They loved hard. My mother would throw herself out in front of a bus to sacrifice her life for her family. Love, food, family and naked Italian statues, these were the things I was raised with.

My high school principal once described me as a very loving, empathetic person, but I had to be conscious of people taking advantage of that. I missed Sister Josephine. I missed high school. I missed how she would curse under her breath in Latin each time I pushed her buttons. I wasn't too sure how I would cope in this wide world. Sister Josephine told me fear was make-believe and it was danger that I had to look out for. She once said my politeness could be perceived as a weakness, so I had to set boundaries with people. I didn't quite understand what she had meant by that. I didn't know what boundaries were.

My mother had taught me to fear nothing, but be smart enough to know when to remove myself from an unhealthy situation and run. I didn't really understand that either. I was raised to be good, that I understood.

As the days went by I began to soften towards Dave. He took an interest in my life and I appreciated it. We would walk to the community library together after work and talk about different novels. He was smart and creative, for an accountant. He would leave funny notes under my car windscreen wipers that made me laugh. He began to dress differently too. We would go shopping together where I would pick out some items for him. He no longer dressed like a golf caddy and more like a sophisticated man. He appreciated and welcomed my suggestions and input. I became important to him and him to me.

I had another friend who would visit me at the deli each Saturday morning. His name was Matteo Famoso. I never told Rosie or Renata about Matteo, the hot Italian-Spaniard. I didn't see a need. Dave was on the scene and I didn't understand choices. I felt like I had none. I was raised with direction. I was told what to do and I followed the rules. I liked Matteo, a lot, but I didn't know if he was a "bad boy" that Rosie would speak of.

Although I didn't sense that with him, I kept thinking to myself I had to keep away. My instincts told me differently, but I ignored them. He made my heart thump in my throat each time he walked through the door. He would make my hands sweat and my face hot. I would become tongue tied and flustered. I would drop things or trip over my feet each time I was around him. I couldn't explain it. I wasn't like this with Dave, it was the opposite. Dave felt familiar and comfortable. Matteo felt more like unchartered waters, not knowing what I might find. He was exciting.

Choice was an inconvenience to my parents. My mother cooked the same meals for the same nights of the week. No choice in what I ate for dinner. No choice where my life headed.

My mother liked Dave. She met him one night and she let me have dinner with him at his favourite restaurant. She liked him because he was a decent man. She said he had kind eyes and you can tell a lot about a person because of them. She also said she could tell how much I meant to him by the way he looked at me. She said that the fact he was pursuing me so hard showed he had spirit and commitment and would fight for me. Not someone who would run away. I didn't tell her it was me doing the running.

My parents had instilled fear into me from a very young age, to protect me. They taught me I had to be 'good'. They force fed me the notion, and when I wasn't 'good' I felt guilty. I was fearful of ever being 'bad' because guilt lingers and rots like an apple at the bottom of your bag.

I was running away from Matteo and into the arms of Dave perhaps because of my guilt. I didn't want to hurt the man who was slowly winning me over with decency and kindness. I didn't need my instincts to tell me what was already there. I could tell, by looking into his eyes.

CHAPTER 10

HALF TRUTHS

I THOUGHT GROWING up in the '70s was hard. I thought I had to fight for my freedom because I had a sheltered, restricted upbringing. I thought the only way through life was to fight. Not a good strategy. Being on guard like an Amazon warrior was exhausting and it would eventually catch up with me.

'Keep expectations and priorities real' became my new mantra. I began to think I had a lot more spirit and determination growing up than I did entering adult hood. Somewhere in-between I had transitioned into a full-blown people pleaser.

Married life to Dave was fantastic. We had settled into our little house and made it our own. It was a simple home filled with my version of love. Our neighbours welcomed us. We were the youngest couple on the block.

I discovered my independence on so many levels. I was making my own decisions and I furthered my education taking night classes at the local high school. Dave worked away and staying home alone was nothing new to me. I grew up alone. Although on occasions I shared many fun times with my cousins, we were all raised alone. We were not accepted by society because we didn't fit the Aussie mould. Making new friends was hard because we were different.

Funnily enough, this is what led me to marrying Dave. He fell in love with me because I was different. He said I wasn't like every other girl he had met. He called me exotic.

82

He said I had vision and spirit and was drawn to me because I had a big heart and lots of love to give. He liked how I took good care of him. He felt very loved and blessed.

Dave even accepted the elaborate over the top wedding. He didn't care we had rules to follow on our day. He accepted my mother's colour schemes and suggestions that were quickly set in stone. She had been planning for my wedding long before Dave came onto the scene. He went along with it. He didn't care we were taped together with paper streamers by our guests on our first dance and had to be cut free. He loved Italian food and his stomach had stretched accordingly to the number of courses served at family gatherings and celebrations. Long gone were the days of ham and cheese toasties he once ate.

My parents had retired and they were travelling back and forth to Italy. They had discovered their next phase in life and came and went as they pleased. Their duty had been seen out. I was palmed off to Dave.

Even though I was married, they still tried having a say in my life. They weren't as intense as they were when I was living at home. They visited me often, but once they left, so did their expectations. I had learnt not to take their suggestions personally. I had discovered my own personal taste. I would close the front door behind them with a smile on my face. I welcomed their holidays away and I encouraged them to go on more. Freedom started to taste amazing.

Friends came and went. I was blessed to have made new ones. They were different from my high school friends. My new friends were more liberated.

Most of the girls from high school had parents who had visions that women should have a little job on the side. Where they could combine motherhood and work once married with children.

I was married, but I viewed the world a little differently to those around me. I preferred to be on the forefront of life. Leading the way for others and changing society's perceptions on what women could do, not what they shouldn't do. My old friends were shed and new ones stepped in and stood beside me to join my journey.

I found my niche on the front lawn, one morning in our local newspaper. I saw an advertisement calling for volunteers. I joined a political community group. I would volunteer my time assisting them with whatever cause we deemed fighting for. I thought it was a good avenue to pursue and surround myself with likeminded people. I enjoyed making a positive contribution to the community.

I was now fighting for different things in life with a support system of new friends. We were all on the same page, sharing similar interests and values. My strength, resilience and determination were assets. People were drawn to me because of them.

There were days I felt like I was a clone of my mother, fearless and confident. This turned Dave on. It lit a spark in him. But there were also days I experienced vulnerability where I would feel the same as I did growing up. Alone.

Taking on extra responsibilities was lonely. Dave's interests lay elsewhere. He found my new interests impacted on our relationship. He found them threatening. Knowledge was power and it took away my time from him. I had spoilt Dave in the early stages of our marriage, making him my first priority. I didn't know any different. Like my older cousin Maria would say, "It's your duty to take care of your husband and family."

I began to learn different things from my new friends. I wanted more out of life and I wanted to share this with the world. I wanted to fix society. I wasn't going to settle for the dutiful housewife tag and scrubbing bathrooms wasn't filling my void. I wasn't happy settling for Mountain White bleach and laundry soap. I wasn't happy staying home making fresh pasta on my weekends off.

I was still working in a deli because I had to contribute to our household expenses. I craved more. I didn't want to be seen like one of the girls from high school where life stopped once I had a ring on my finger. I had a burning desire for change. I had visions of working fulltime where I could campaign for change and people would take notice.

Dave and I had decided to try for a baby. Getting him on-board was difficult. He was more interested in planning for our financial future, which was his domain, to be fair. I guess I was like him too in a sense, but I planned for others, not us. I couldn't see this at the time. Like Dave, I hadn't known how crucial it was to stop and embrace the moment.

Becoming pregnant wasn't hard at all. We worked around Dave's time away from home. I had convinced myself it wouldn't happen instantly, but it did. Boom, in no time I had discovered I had a little peanut growing inside of me.

Balancing motherhood, our relationship, and political ideologies became an even bigger challenge. Themes from my high school days seemed to follow me into my adulthood. This time I wasn't singing the National Anthem each week at assembly. I was singing a different tune. I was proud of the country I called home, my birthplace, the same endearment I felt towards school. I stood proud and patriotic. Although shunned by the pupils, I still held my head high. Now I was still being shunned by others because of my gender. Even from the same gender! I found it difficult to understand.

Dave told me once he thought I lived in a bubble. I couldn't fight for something that had already been predetermined by society. But I had an even bigger reason to try.

I had my little bumble bee to think of. I wanted her to be able to hold her head up high too and not face the same challenges I once did. I was laying the path for her to take her journey on and making it easier.

I was a young mum, giving birth to Chloe on Good Friday. She was ten days late. My little screamer was born free. No expectations and certainly not force-fed traditions. Chloe had the greenest eyes and fair skin. She reminded me of Renata, a free spirit. And of Rosie, clever enough to recognise danger from a young age. It didn't take her long to learn if you touch something hot you will get burnt. And life had a way of disguising these lessons.

My best friend Dina Williams also had a child the same age as Chloe. We had decided our life purpose included children and their future lay in our hands. We had an obligation and responsibility to make this world a better place for them to live in.

I met Dina when I was taking night classes. We were both newlyweds with a lot in common. We promised to be there for one another, regardless. She was an Aussie, but treated everyone the same. She accepted me for who I was.

Dina had a way of keeping me grounded. She was a good listener and offered me genuine advice. When this didn't work, she would threaten to slap me. It worked and seemed to snap me back into reality. Reminiscent of the five fingered, one handed schiaffi (slaps) we'd get as kids, quickly snapping us out of it.

When our children were young, we began having different catch up sessions working around our families. We began our own tradition.

We lived in the same neighbourhood and would make time to walk in the evenings together once everyone had been fed and settled. Walking and talking had become our counselling sessions where we could offload to one another. Sharing our desires and deepest secrets was our therapy.

We had decided there were certain things our husbands didn't need to know. We promised to only share these with one another. Gone were the days we relied heavily on our men for conversations and including them in everything we did. We once lived for them, but we were now living for many things. We were mothers and sometimes we had to plan to get what we wanted. Sometimes you must enter via the back door instead of the front. Our problem solving had become inventive and successful.

Like my mother once said, "Watch what you feed your husbands. Stick with food to fill their stomachs, not unnecessary chatter that fill their heads with doubt. Save your conversation for your friends and there are certain things you keep to yourself. Allowing for a peaceful relationship and marriage. They read into things that don't concern them! Men are fixers, sometimes women just want to be heard, not fixed. Pick up the phone and call a friend instead."

I learnt a lot from the women in my life, especially my mother. Men believed anything she fed them.

CHAPTER 11

NEW ERA OF SELF-HELP

Walking and talking was my remedy to a happy marriage. Dave hated coming home and finding me on the phone talking to my friends. He would say I was choosing them over him. Why was it that he could take phone calls, but I couldn't? Dina had the same problem. She had to sneak into another room to take my calls so her husband wouldn't hear her. At times, I felt no different to when I was a teenager, stretching the handset into the bathroom for a private chat. Dina and I began to save what we had to say for our walks.

"What a beautiful night for a walk, I love spring. It's my favourite season," I said.

Dina and I were briskly walking side by side. We passed homes where we could see families sitting at their table eating dinner through their front window.

"Me too, I can't wait for summer," she said.

"Em, I've been really tired lately, I have so much on my plate at the moment. There are days I don't feel like getting out of bed. I have so much to contend with and I don't know where to start. Sometimes I wish I'd get hit by a car so I don't have to face my responsibilities!" Dina said.

"Dina, what are you talking about? Don't say things like that, don't you know that what you put out there you get back?" I scolded.

"Life's hard Em, I'm tired. Darren comes home and expects dinner ready. He came home the other day to find me sitting down and he had the nerve to ask what I had been doing all day. It's always a criticism with him," she said.

"I had only just finished cooking dinner and sat down to fold the washing at the dining table. I'm over having to justify to him what I do. I actually apologised. Sorry came out of my mouth before I'd even realised! It naturally rolled off my tongue," Dina said.

"We all have days like that. Don't feel guilty or apologise for sitting down, who cares what Darren thinks! You don't have to justify yourself to him about housework. I'm surprised you're taking this to heart, normally you would have shut him down quick smart," I said.

"You can talk! You work fulltime and feel guilty for not being at home for Chloe. You overcompensate with giving to Dave. I've seen you go home and bake cakes and thank him for mopping the floors! You ask what he'd like for dessert. He said carrot cake before he even emptied the mop bucket! Going the extra mile to ask you to ice it with cream cheese. You'll crash and burn one day you know!" she said.

Dina was right. Dave said carrot cake faster than he emptied the water out of the bucket. I did thank Dave for helping me out. I shouldn't have thanked him. I shouldn't have baked that bloody carrot cake either. He didn't thank me for cooking and cleaning and the one time I handed him a mop and bucket I was indebted to him. What was my problem? Did I feel guilty? I deserved help around the home. I was working and raising our child. I wasn't a single parent, but I felt like one. This was supposed to be a team effort.

We walked in silence for a moment, both thinking and taking in the scent of food cooking around us as we passed more homes.

"Sometimes I feel like I deserve better, sometimes I wished my life was different. I love Dave, I love being a mum, but

God he annoys me sometimes and he's like a fucking baby. Is this what I've created for myself?" I asked.

Dina smirked, "I do think about what it would be like to sleep with another man at times, someone hot. I've started to fantasise during sex because Darren reminds me of a fucking baby too," we both laughed.

"I knew a hot guy once, before I met Dave. His name was Matteo. Sex with him was awesome, off this planet," I said.

Dina stopped, grabbing my arm and looking at me.

"Who, what?" she asked.

I filled Dina in as we walked. I had never shared my story about Matteo with anyone before and it felt good. I actually felt like I had done something bad in life. I felt empowered. My little secret, with memories that I owned.

"Do you think people have affairs because they're burnt out or feel like they deserve something better out of life?" she asked.

"Maybe. I also think it's about the underlying emotional intimacy too. It could be as simple as someone complimenting them instead of criticising and taking the time to listen. Feeling beautiful again and having someone appreciate you on an entirely different level, instead of asking what time dinner is. It could also be about sexual empowerment and feeling sexually liberated with another man. Why, are you planning on having one?" I asked.

She smiled.

"I don't condone it, but who am I to judge? I've got my hands full so it's not ever going to be an option for me. I get by with our friendship, our walks and I would rather connect deeply with my favourite baked cheesecake with a serve of fresh whipped cream and strawberries on the side," she said and we laughed.

"Why didn't you go with Matteo? What made you choose Dave?" she asked.

"Because I was raised to do the right thing, and Dave, that pain-in-the-arse, was persistent. I reckon he fell in love with my tortellini all panna and not me," I joked.

"Do you know what my biggest struggle in life has been?" I asked Dina.

"No, what?" she replied.

"Overthinking. My mind. Identifying with the only relationship that I was raised with, and groomed to be a wife and mother. Not encouraged to have one with myself. I feel like I have missed out on life in the sense I wasn't given options to explore or achieve greater things. I had to settle for marriage and kids, not that I'm ungrateful, but what if I was given the opportunity to pursue university? What if I had a degree like Rosie, and moved interstate? Sometimes when I reminisce about my life, I begin to think about the 'what-ifs'."

"Yeah, I understand, at least you ended up with a good job," she said.

"I love working as a community liaison officer. I love writing proposals for improvement for our area. I still feel empty though. I want another child as well. I don't want Chloe missing out like I did," I said.

"It has to start with me though, because I don't know who 'me' actually is! Sometimes I get frustrated with Dave for leaving wet towels on the bathroom floor, but deep down I don't really care. Sometimes I get angry just for the sake of it. But when I stop and think about why I get angry, it's really because I'm so pissed off that he has his shit together and I don't. He's recognised by others for the work that he does, he's appreciated, he's a man, and he's the breadwinner.

Deep down, all I really want is his attention, appreciation and recognition for what I do," I said.

"Don't you think we all do? At least you had a taste of attention when we went to night school. Do you remember Dimitri? He couldn't get enough of you," she reminded me.

"Gee, now there's a name I haven't heard in a long while! My little Greek lamb, Dimitri Panaganis. I haven't seen him in years. Thanks for the reminder, but he's not quite the 'taste' I'm looking for. God, I haven't been able to look at yiros the same since Dimitri. He'd always slap on extra tzatziki and it would repeat on me."

"I wonder what ever happened to him?" she asked.

"He was always trying to convince the world how cool he was. Back in the day he could get away with it, but hopefully he's moved beyond his informal teens and finally transitioned into adult-hood," I said.

"Why don't you send him an email and see how he's doing? To appease our curiosity and find out where he's at in life," Dina suggested.

"To appease *yours*, you mean. I don't know, I don't think it's a good idea to open that door, I really see no point. If I'm meant to see him again, it will happen. Don't you know the universe only sends us what we can handle? I've still got all my faculties at the moment, so I'll pass on the email for now."

"Universal law, hey? Reading another self-help book then?" she asked with a cheeky grin.

CHAPTER 12

CONTROL ALT DELETE

Technology was moving at such a rapid pace it became easier to replace items than to get them fixed. Some technicians struggled to keep up with the constant updates. No sooner would they get their heads around one product, the next version was released. It was jumping ahead and the teething process threw a lot of people out of sync. A little like relationships. Life was once simple.

Xavier Julius was introduced to the world on Christmas Day. I couldn't have been more Christian if I tried, having each child born on a significant holy day.

Chloe had her first mobile phone at age ten, because she had to walk to and from school with her little brother. XJ was in good hands with his older sister. XJ looked up to Chloe. She knew if she encountered danger, she could take out her phone and dial for help. Her device made her feel safe and secure. Kids were becoming so technologically savvy, bypassing adults who relied heavily on reading manuals and instructions. We were now relying on children to help us understand technology.

XJ had introduced me to many new things in my life. Juggling more than one child and forging new friendships. Because of XJ, I had a new job and new best friends.

Due to our work schedules, Dave and I didn't have time for school drop-offs and pickups. Dave had become a successful accountant. He ran his own business and bought an office in the city. I was working for a female politician, fighting for women's rights. Better pay conditions and maternity cover within the workforce.

I loved my job and it was everything I ever dreamt of. It filled my void and offered me a distraction. I preferred to keep myself busy. If I ever stopped, it would force me to look within and I was scared at what would I find. I wasn't ready to address my issues. I guess I was too busy creating a beautiful career and not a beautiful marriage.

I was seeking outside validation through my role at work. People looked up to me and respected me. I hadn't yet worked out it was my limiting beliefs that were leading me to look outside and not within. It takes more strength to stop running and searching than it does to distract yourself. I was a great people watcher, but not when it came to people watching me.

Sharni Kendall was my best friend. We met when she was working at a women's centre where I too eventually gained employment. Our careers were shared as were our political beliefs and it felt good being on the same page as someone else. Sharni was a kindhearted humanitarian. She saw the good in people and although she also saw the bad, she would choose her words wisely when it came to describing them. She was a petite Malaysian woman who had an artistic streak. She wore brightly-coloured eyewear frames and organic cotton shirts. She had a dry sense of humour and was one of the very few people who could make me laugh hard. I liked sharing my office space with her.

Sharni took her laptop out of her bag, "Hey Em, you didn't tell me Jess split with her husband?" she asked.

We had arrived at work before anyone else. Preferring to get a head start before the phones began ringing.

"I saw she changed her relationship status from 'married' to 'single'. What happened?" she inquired.

Jess Thompson was a mutual friend of ours. She worked as a beauty therapist and her son Sam attended the same school as Chloe and XJ. Sam and XJ were the same age. Jess and I would have our regular catch ups, drinking and going out to see live bands. Sharni would join us when she could.

It became much easier to make friends nowadays. You pulled out your phone and hit send, voilà, a new friend! But I still preferred to keep my friends real and not from the internet.

Jess had confided in me she was struggling with her marriage. Her struggles were familiar to most women. Some found ways around them and chose to stay for the sake of their children. Some stay because of the financial restrictions. Some stay because they have nowhere else to go.

I understood from a personal level. I had marital problems, but I chose wisely who I shared my struggles with and it certainly was not online. Behind a fight or a break-up, you will find a reason. My reasons were always the same. Alcohol. Although I would forgive Dave the following day and move on, the 'reason' still remained.

"She told me she caught Geoff chatting online with another woman. This woman also sent nude photos of herself to him. Apparently, it's not the first time he's done this," I explained.

"Are you serious? What's going on with this world, they seemed like such a lovely couple," Sharni said.

"I guess you never know what really goes on behind closed doors. She was always posting nice family photos online. Maybe she was trying to convince herself she had the perfect little family," Sharni said.

"Maybe a little time apart is what she needs, he's moved out, he's staying at a mates place for the time being," I said.

"Apparently, he blamed Jess. He said it was because she was always tired and gave him little attention. I've got this feeling he will eventually move in with this woman. I don't know why, but my gut is telling me he will."

"So, it's her fault?" Sharni asked.

"Apparently. I guess the real reason he was cheating was because he thought he could get away with it. He's telling people it's because she's not giving him attention and she's always working, and has *issues*."

"Issues? What does that even mean these days? The word 'issues' is so broad. We all have issues!" Sharni said.

"She's tried hard to keep her family together. She doesn't want some other woman stepping into her home or her child's life. She sees her role as a wife and mother, but she's more than that and can't see it. This could break her you know. We need to keep an eye on her. She needs our support we don't want her losing herself altogether," I said.

"I feel it's so much easier to be replaced these days. Instead of growing within a relationship, people are choosing to leave," I said.

"It's become all too easy to meet people online. Jess said the selfies she found weren't of their faces either."

"What a moron. He's not a horny teenager," Sharni said.

"Loving someone is like learning a magic trick," I said.

"How so?" Sharni asked.

"It takes skill to love someone. You have times that you fail, but you learn with practice. Relationships need cultivating, attention and care. A balance of practice and gratitude. It takes real strength to master them simultaneously. Every relationship has shitty moments. If you can pull it off, you'll begin to see what you have instead of focusing on what you don't. You'll experience real magic between two people. It becomes easier to focus on the negatives, which justify walking away. Some people choose to walk. That's society's problem, we're becoming fucking lazy in relationships when it becomes difficult to manage. A bunch of quitters. Or maybe some have become so desensitised by life they don't give a shit and their tolerance becomes a lot lower. Maybe if Geoff chose to look at all the things Jess *did* do and showed a bit of gratitude, she would feel appreciated. But he's looking at what she doesn't do. He's taken the glass half empty approach, when he should be grateful to have a glass in the first place."

"What love represents to one person, might not be the same to the other. Maybe if they both sought some counselling then they can determine what love means to them," I said.

"It starts within, he's looking for outside validation to fill his glass. He's not practicing respectfulness at all, and she's left drowning in confusion and hurt," I said.

"Mm. How are things with you and Dave going?" she asked.

"I bit like swimming," I said with a smirk.

"Waiting for that tidal-wave to hit unexpectedly."

"I'm happy to support Dave as best as I can. But I won't compromise my sanity for him. When he becomes too much, I'll let him know. I'll help him as much as I can, but he's going to have to help himself first. You can't flog a dead horse. People need to learn from their own mistakes and choices in life."

Sharni read something from her laptop.

"Hey, there's a concert in the park coming up, we should take Jess. I reckon she could use a night out. I should buy tickets," she suggested.

I walked over to her desk and looked at the post she had up on her computer.

"Sounds like a great idea! Let's go!" I said.

"Dave, is Emmie home?"

I thought I heard Jess' voice outside as I approached the front door. Dave was out the front gardening and Jess stood by the door looking teary and upset.

"Jess, come in, what's going on?" I asked as I lead her into the kitchen.

I sat her down and turned on the kettle.

"It's Geoff, he came over this morning. He was begging me to take him back. He was crying and slumped himself on the floor in the lounge room. He was a mess. He said he missed me and he loved me," she said.

"I told him I was sick of his cheating and all the lies. He said I was being too sensitive about it all. He said I should find it in my heart to forgive him, because that's what a kind-hearted wife would do," she said.

"Is that so?" I asked.

"Yes, he's like a broken record because that's what he said the last time too."

Dave walked into the kitchen from the front garden. He had his gardening clothes on, ripped jeans and a black windcheater. He had little bits of green leaves stuck to his top. I looked at him and for a moment and I captured the man I remembered falling in love with. He still looked as handsome as ever. He had a worried look on his face.

"Is everything alright in here?" he asked.

"Yes Dave, thanks for checking. We're having a private moment over tea. Would you like a cup? I'll bring it out to you if you want one," I asked.

"All good, I just thought I'd check," he said, as he patted Jess on the shoulder and walked out.

I handed Jess her cup and a box of tissues.

She looked exhausted and lost. Her eyes were red raw from crying. Someone who always dressed impeccably now looked dishevelled.

"Em, I found Geoff's old phone from two years ago. I charged it up and read all his text messages he had sent to this woman. I looked back at the ones he sent me and I think he may have sent some as a mistake. Telling me he loved me and missed me while I was at work. Then in another one he asked for a cheeky photo. All the while I thought they were for me, but thinking now, I've realised they were for her. I was too busy with clients to question it. I had no reason to," she said sobbing.

"So the idiot couldn't even hit send to the right person," I said.

"Is it the same woman he was caught out with last time?" I asked.

"I think so, but there were lots of messages and emails, that's why I lost it at him when he came over. I'm almost certain there were more women. I found it too overwhelming to go through them all. I'm not coping with any of this," she said.

I could tell Jess wasn't coping. Who would cope? Her desperation and need for answers were painful to watch. How could she ever trust him or anyone else again?

She took more tissues and blew her nose.

"The worst part is, he said if I don't take him back, he will make my life hell. He said he will tell people our breakup was my fault, and that no one will believe me. He said he will tell people I'm a hopeless mother, a dumb beauty therapist and I'll never aspire to be anything more," she said sobbing loudly.

"He said the reason he's the way he is and he's done these things is because I lower his motivation to want to do anything with his life. He said it's my fault, because I'm useless and boring."

I went up to her and put my arm around her.

"Jess, you know that's not true what he says about you. He's playing with your head. Can you see what picture he's trying to paint here? He's trying to make you look like the problem. He's planting the seed of doubt in your mind to try and gaslight you. There are genuine, decent guys out there, you deserve better," I enforced.

"All I know is Sam won't have a loving home and his dad is living at a mate's house. He keeps asking when daddy is coming home."

"Jess, you told me once Geoff was irresponsible with money, that he was an impulsive buyer and gambler. You run a successful small business and you're good at budgeting. You have good friends around who will help you get through this," I said, giving her a big hug.

"Things will get better with time. I promise. They seem bad now, but with time, help and support you will get through this," I said.

"It might seem like you're in a dark place now, but that won't last forever."

"I hope so. I worry about Sam. I worry about the uncertainty in my life. I don't know anything different than being a mum and a wife," she said.

"You have to be you first. You will always be Sam's mum, but find who Jess is first. Don't settle for second best. Be a happier version of you," I said.

"Don't rely on a man to provide you with self-worth, find it within you!"

"Love is more than red roses and French Champagne. It's a commitment to one another, both emotionally and physically," I said.

As the days went by, I thought of ways to help Jess. I had even mapped out a plan. Baby steps, Sharni was on board. We were due to fly to Melbourne. We were taking Jess with us for the weekend and we were staying with Rosie. We needed the sisterhood to come together and come up with ideas to bring about a smooth resolution and transition for Jess. I had experienced with women I assisted through work that calm forward planning was the best way to forge ahead.

It forced me to reflect on my relationship with Dave and how it was slowly crumbling away, like sticking a fork into a dry, hard chocolate cake. There's no coming back from dry cake, you have to bin it and start over. I thought of my life and how I was constantly searching for my purpose, but maybe my purpose was already staring at me in the face.

Was there an expectation on women to marry and have children? Was this societies expectation or my own? Was I fighting a losing battle? Who was I even up against? What was I supposed to learn? I was good at giving advice to others. I had drawn up a plan for Jess, but my own map looked like it had more roadblocks than freeways. I thought of the highs and lows I'd had with Dave over the years. We seemed to work our way through our relationship dilemmas, mainly because I was so forgiving and selectively forgetful.

Some women were fearful of losing the familiarity of their relationships. Some feared having to move out and make it on their own. Some feared being alone forever. Uncertainty seemed to be the biggest fear of all.

I thought of the stories I had read as a child, all with the same happy endings and their Prince Charming. Is this where I developed my idealism of what my life should be like as an adult? Was Dave my Prince Charming? Did he rescue or fix me? Did the story book Prince Charming consume high volumes of alcohol? I couldn't think of anything more disappointing, having to rely on a man in my life. I didn't need a man to rescue me. I was in control of my life. I wanted a man who showed me appreciation and acknowledgment. I felt like the scales were tipping more to Dave's side instead of a perfect equilibrium. We lived in a modern society, yet women were still disadvantaged, even in their relationships. There had to be a middle ground.

CHAPTER 13

DRY HONEY ROASTED

GROWING UP IN my household, there were never dirty dishes found in the kitchen sink. No sooner was your plate empty, it was taken from you and washed immediately, then put away. There was never an opportunity to see mess. My mother didn't have a dishwasher, I was her dishwasher. I ate fast and regardless of how hot the food was, I never burnt myself. The kitchen sink was filled with boiling soapy water to ensure the plates were squeaky clean. My hands became accustomed to extreme heat from a very young age.

I didn't have time to savour and appreciate food like Dave did. He would take his time eating. It was frustrating to watch. Sunday lunches at my parents' home were always animated. If it wasn't my mother arguing with my father over what time lunch was served, it would be me and Dave. I wanted to wash the dishes and leave straight after. I didn't want to spend my only free day sitting around the dining table watching him eat chicken, stripping every last piece of meat off the bones. I had never actually seen white chicken bones before I had met Dave. He ate every last scrap. I was always in a hurry. He said I should take my time and stop wasting good food. I'd take one bite of my chicken leg and the rest went in the bin.

Some days Dave would come and see me at work and take me out for lunch. I liked when he did this. I was secretly proud to show him off to the others in the office. I didn't have to post him online. I'd never let on I felt this way, but I did. He was good looking. He dressed sophisticated. He had a dry sense of humour and made all the other girls laugh, without even trying. He wasn't someone who had to be the centre of attention, he was the opposite. He was humble and kind and he fit in well with others, regardless of who they were. He was a great listener and always polite with a smile on his face. In fact, he was always smiling because he said that life had been kind to him and he was grateful.

Dave and I weren't opposites. I wasn't a believer in the cliché 'opposites attract'. If you want a successful relationship, then you have to share commonalities in morals and priorities. It's those core blocks that keep couples stable. We weren't soul mates either, we were great mates. I wasn't a believer in some universal umbilical cord attaching you to one individual. I had lots of mates and I didn't have to be spiritually attached to any of them. I loved them and I expressed this in a natural manner, with respect and personal boundaries.

Someone in my office had developed a crush on Dave. I was surprised she had the nerve to tell me. At first, I was taken aback, but then I appreciated her honesty. I took it as a compliment, although my mother disagreed with me when I mentioned it to her. She called her a "puttana (slut)" and told me I had to clean up the mess. But I looked at the situation a little less dramatically. I didn't see a mess at all. I certainly didn't see the need to cut off a horse's head, sneak into her home and lay it beside her in bed whilst she slept.

I preferred to think Dave's infatuated crush gave me an upper hand to sit back and watch. She thought she was in with a real shot, if I wasn't on the scene. But I was on the scene. I was the director and casting agent. Another nut I was forced to encounter in life, for reasons yet to be determined.

I went home that evening and asked Dave straight away. Dave was sitting in the lounge room watching his regular evening news.

"Dave, did you say anything to Tara about liking her? She told me today that you said you fancied her?" I asked him.

Dave looked surprised. He picked up the television remote control from the coffee table and turned the volume down.

"No, I didn't say anything like that. She asked if a guy like me would date someone like her and I said yes to be polite. I felt very awkward that a stranger would ask me a question like that," he said with a worried look on his face.

"I'm not interested in anyone but you," he added.

I knew this already. Dave wouldn't intentionally hurt me and it was his politeness or his ignorance that got him in trouble at times. Women liked Dave, because he was too polite. Dave didn't want to hurt anyone's feelings, regardless of gender.

Tara was annoying. She had burgundy coloured hair with a straight cut fringe and freckles. She was large with a beer barrel belly. She was a bombastic and loud woman who liked to drink. She always drenched herself heavily in cheap floral perfume. She liked to wear heavy purple shiny eyeshadow and bright purple lipstick. Her strap on sandals never really matching her flowing skirts that she would layer different coloured tops over. She was the only person who did any work in our office, apparently. She was someone who had her fingers in every pie and miraculously grew more when more pies were baked. She would often huff and puff around the office because she was always the busiest. We would all roll our eyes at her self-promoting. Her micromanaging drove us all up the wall, she just couldn't help herself sticking her nose in everyone's business.

Tara's confession wasn't really something you'd say to a friend, never mind a work colleague. She had no integrity or boundaries. She saw herself somewhat as a sex symbol, but the overconfidence smacked of deep-seeded insecurities.

I didn't like how she spoke about Dave around me. She was trying to push my buttons. I stood back and I observed her actions just like my mother had raised me to, with sophistication and class. My mother was an expert at cleaning up messes.

Jealousy makes people do crazy things. Tara began texting Dave. He showed me, he wasn't the one who had anything to hide. We trusted one another. He made subtle suggestions to Tara where she could go to meet available men, someone who wasn't already taken. Then he blocked her number.

There was a man in our office who actually liked Tara, but she brushed him off, labelling him as boring and old. She was too busy chasing her own make-believe.

Dave was coming in to take me out to lunch. A new bakery had opened its doors up the road and the smell of fresh pastries was too good to resist.

Tara had decided she was taking her lunch break at the same time as me so she could join us. There's nothing quite like watching an uninvited third wheel. Desperation could be pitiful at times. I decided to take a back seat. I felt like I was watching a tennis match, the competition was between Tara and herself. She was too busy trying to impress Dave and kick me to the curb.

"I'll have a steak and mushroom pie, thanks."

Dave eagerly placed his order at the counter.

"I'll have the same!" Tara exclaimed.

I could tell he was feeling awkward. I was secretly laughing to myself. I should have ordered popcorn instead of a pie.

"I'll go see what's taking so long," I said, standing up.

The pies arrived in brown paper bags, placed down on our table.

Tara took a big bite of her pie and the filling spilled onto her chin. There was steam coming out of the pastry like you would see coming out of an Italian's ears and nose when they were angry.

She instantly dropped her pie, her chin was red, as was her face.

"This pie is HOT!" she cried.

I sat there quietly eating my pie watching. It was hot, but I liked hot things. I could handle hot well. Tara couldn't, she was an amateur.

"Tara, are you okay? Let me get you some water," Dave said, racing up to grab a bottle from the counter.

Dave poured some water onto a paper napkin and handed it to Tara so she could place it on her red chin. She was patting it down.

Whilst the commotion continued, I happily finished my pie and extra hot latte. I got up to leave, I kissed Dave goodbye and told Tara I'd see her back at the office and I left. My stomach was happily full.

I wasn't threatened by Tara. I was disappointed to think another woman would feel so jealous of my life that it would make her behave in a way that would jeopardise a working relationship. Women were supposed to stick together in this world, be familiar with the sisterhood. Why was this nut trying to seep into my life? I had forged my own path. She was a fool to think she had an opportunity to step in, because the opportunity was never there to begin with. I had to pretend to be a fool in order to trick the fool who thought she was fooling me. I was always miles ahead of Tara.

Dave never once gave me any reason to feel insecure because true love meant the same thing to us both. Love isn't only about attraction and chemistry. Genuine love takes time to develop. It's like a good Italian vino, the relationship requires nurturing. It's tried and tested over time. Love isn't found through idealisation, that's not real. It's about a mutual tolerance and respect towards one another. You don't turn the tap on and off when life becomes tough. It's about bettering oneself. It's about integrity and honesty.

Dave had never been fearful of sharing anything with me. We both knew we could address anything without judgement or blame. Love doesn't give you psychic powers to read minds, communication is the key to unlock insecurities and lay these to rest. Acceptance is true love, and gratitude is found from it.

I used to feel sad for women like Tara once, but I no longer did. She made little meringue cookies as office gifts, perhaps as a gesture to seek attention from others. Showing off her culinary skills, she liked to think of herself as a gourmet chef. She had left a few on my desk tied up in cellophane paper. I took the little parcel and stomped on it when she had left for the day. It felt so good feeling the meringue crush beneath my foot and then I put it in the bin. I didn't need her cookies.

I had someone who loved me for me. Even on bad days. I was blessed. Like a good Italian, I cleaned up the mess before anyone saw it. Or perhaps even realised. Move the obstropolous along.

CHAPTER 14

MR MRS MISS MS OTHER

WHEN XJ WAS little, his favourite Sunday morning breakfast was pancakes. He would call them patacake. We would get up and make them together. He would happily watch the batter bubble up in the hot pan and flip them over until they were cooked through. We would then spread the table out with different condiments: Canadian maple syrup, real butter, homemade strawberry jam and cream.

As Chloe grew older, she preferred to make healthier versions and would cook her own pancakes made with chia seeds and coconut flour. Her taste buds changed according to the latest food fads and what was in fashion at the time.

Today was special. Renata was joining us for Sunday morning pancakes. Renata had lived interstate for a few years. She too chose Rosie's path. Renata was living in Brisbane, regularly travelling to different states to chase her dream.

She was an artist, returning home every six months or so to catch up with family.

Today, Chloe and XJ had decided they were making carob banana pancakes served with organic yogurt and fresh blueberries. They were excited to see Renata again.

"HEY!" Renata yelled, as she ran up and hugged them.

"XJ, I feel like I'm going to put my neck out trying to kiss you, how tall are you? Chloe, you are as beautiful as ever. I have missed you both so much!" she exclaimed.

Renata handed them both a t-shirt she had made. They had the slogan: 'Keep things real' on the front. She was working at a screen printer and she was selling her artwork at various markets on the weekends. She was wearing one of her designs, a red and white tie-dye t-shirt over black skinny leg jeans and a multi-coloured headband.

Keeping in touch these days wasn't hard at all. Just about everyone video called or spoke over social media.

Dave was completely out of touch with 'reality', refusing to have a social media account. Who could blame him really, the world was turning upside-down. He chose simple and uncomplicated, without the digital disruptions.

"Dave, you look good for a Sunday morning," Renata said.

Renata and Dave both shared the same dry sense of humour. They liked to tease one another. Dave walked up to her and gave her a big hug and kiss.

Renata hadn't met anyone yet. She preferred to be in platonic relationships. She wasn't someone who would settle down and commit to one person. We accepted her as she was, she was family and she was loved. She filled us in on her adventures over breakfast. Her stories were always entertaining and left us in fits of laughter. She was a risk taker. She wasn't backwards in coming forwards when it came to cutting ties with the unwanted in her life. 'Move the fuck along' was her mantra.

"Ren, tell us some stories. Are you seeing anyone at the moment?" I asked.

"I was, just up until recently. I met this guy at a music festival. We had been seeing one another on and off for about four months. I was attracted to him, but the sex was terrible. He's only forty, but has the body of a sixty-year-old. It was sag bags all over the place. I didn't know what I was feeling at times, no wonder he insisted on the lights being off," she said.

"Ren please! Kids cover your ears!" I laughed.

"So, I guess you've decided not to see him anymore?" I asked.

"Correct. He's a strange one. He added me to social media straight away and he was tagging me in all sorts of shit. I had to block him in the end. It became all too hard. He would post stuff and pretend like I was there with him when I wasn't. He took photos of me and then posted them without my permission," she said.

"According to his profile we were in a relationship. He creeped me out."

"That's why I'm not online, more trouble than its worth," Dave pipped up.

"Dave, I'm starting to think after all these years you might actually be right for once. I wouldn't normally admit that," she smiled.

I smiled. Dave was right. He seemed to get himself in enough trouble as it was without the online exposure. Women liked him because he was a genuinely nice guy. Dave had his own sex appeal without having to post it. He already owned it.

I looked over at Dave as he began to clear the dishes away from the table. He had a navy-blue v neck sweater on and dark blue skinny jeans. He looked hot. He was always well dressed. I looked at XJ and Chloe, and I smiled to myself. I was proud of them all.

"Ren, why are you and mum so different?" XJ asked.

"We're not really. We do have the same green eyes and physical features. We grew up with the same traditions. We'd do anything for our families. The only difference is your mum has a lot of patience and is very forgiving. She holds onto many of the traditions instilled into her as a child. She's a leader in her own right. I'm a lover not a fighter and I like having lots of those too. I don't want to settle down just yet. I'm a free spirit."

"Dave, I can't believe you're clearing dishes and tidying up. Isn't that woman's work?" Renata asked trying to bait him.

"Good try, Ren! It's not a big deal. I do my bit to help. Some choose to live in a traditional household, what does that matter? Em and I do what works for us. If the dishes need washing, I'll do them," he said.

"Em, you've trained him well," Renata said.

"No training required, he was already well equipped," I said winking at her.

"Yeah, I understand what you're saying, Dave. I get confused when I go out to dinner with guys. I don't know who's supposed to pay anymore?" Renata said.

"You should do what feels comfortable for you. If you want to pay half then do it. It shouldn't matter if you're male or female. My mum took on both roles when dad died and we all helped her, so there were no blurred lines for us. If I had to wash clothes and scrub bathrooms, I did. You'd know Renata, you pretty much had the same deal," Dave said.

"Yeah, I watched many primadonna moments when my mum and sister had meltdowns. We had lots of arguments in our home. My sister was very dominating towards me. Some days my mother would argue with her and other days she would agree with her," she said.

"At times it felt like mum would play one off against the other and I'd feel guilty for not helping out as much as Maria did."

"Our parents certainly knew how to manipulate certain situations. Not everything should be an argument or drama," I said.

I got up and walked over to Dave who was standing at the kitchen sink. I put my arms around him and hugged him. He turned around and kissed me.

"Gross, can you keep your bedroom actions for behind closed doors," Chloe piped up.

"There's nothing wrong with loving your father, Chloe," I said.

Renata turned to Chloe and XJ who were still sitting at the dining table.

"You guys are both very lucky to be raised in a modern household. I would have given anything to see my mum put her arms around my dad."

"Remember family gatherings Ren? We couldn't join in like we do today," I reminded her.

"Yes as kids we weren't allowed to sit at the main table with the adults. We had to sit at the kids table until we were thirteen! We sat on little chairs and ate at the coffee table. One day one of the plastic chairs gave way under Rosie and we were upgraded to the adult table," she said.

I began to laugh.

"I don't think my kids could grasp what it was like for us growing up. Making allowances, following rules, constantly being told what to do," I said.

"You're blessed to have a mum and dad who love one another and love you both very much. They've both committed in giving you the best out of life. My dad passed away when I was seven so I didn't have a male role model. I didn't go to university. I really didn't apply myself much at all. I was always looking for direction and trying to fit in. I lost myself in the process. Instead of my mum encouraging me, she would put a negative spin on anything I wanted to try. It was always about others and their perceptions. Kids, you are both supported and encouraged to have opinions and choices. You have parents that don't expect you to meet someone and marry them. There's no fake or make-believe in this household. You've both got the real deal and real is rare, remember that," Renata said.

CHAPTER 15

DEMENTED BOREDOM

I DIALLED DINA'S number from my work desk. My colleagues were getting ready for Friday night drinks. Some were making their way into the staff kitchen and coming out with bottles of white wine and glasses, clinking away. It was the culture to finish off the week with a few too many. Is this all we had to look forward to after a long week at work? I couldn't think of anything worse. I already spent far too much time at work that kept me away from my family and my home.

I heard Dina on the other end, "Hey, how's it going?"

"Hi, what are you up to tonight?" I asked.

"The usual, cook dinner and hang out with Darren. Nothing new, why?" she asked.

"Dave's going to the pub and I want to go out. I'm sick of staying home on a Friday night when everyone else is out having drinks and dinner after work. I've had a full-on week. I want to go out for dinner and a few drinks," I said.

Dave spent more and more time at the pub these days and I was sick of it. He said it was because he couldn't deal with the stress from work. He couldn't deal with the volume of work. He couldn't deal with much at all, actually. His de-stress was alcohol. He once said I put my friends before him, but now he was doing the same to me. I saw his drinking as an avoidance to spending time with me, or to address his deep-seated issues. I missed him.

I didn't want to stay back at the office and drink after a long week. I wanted to go home and see Dave, but he wasn't around.

"I'm sorry, Em. I promised Darren I'd stay in tonight and watch a movie with him," she said.

"I understand. Raincheck?" I asked.

"Sure," she replied.

I hung up the phone disappointed. I wanted to do normal things like my friends did. I wanted to put on my pyjamas, order a pizza and snuggle up to Dave on the sofa and watch a movie. I thought about ringing Dave and hoping for a response other than the one I always got. I bit the bullet and dialled his number.

"Hello, Em."

"Dave, I'd really like to go out to dinner tonight. Can we please go together?" I asked.

"Em, what's up, everything okay?" he asked.

"Yeah, everything is fine. I just want to eat out tonight," I said.

"I guess so, why don't you swing by the pub and pick me up at 8 o'clock and we can go from there?" he suggested.

"8 o'clock is too late to eat. Don't worry about it. See you at home later," I said shortly then hung up.

Ordinarily I wouldn't care, but tonight was different. It was our wedding anniversary and Dave had completely forgotten. Alcoholics are forgetful.

In a normal relationship, 8 o'clock would have been a good compromise. I had time and it wasn't a big deal. But I knew he would be completely smashed by 8 o'clock and that's not someone I'd want to be sitting down to share a meal or conversation with.

Dave didn't know how to handle his alcohol. He didn't know when to stop. It was a turn off. I wanted to share my life with someone other than an alcoholic. I felt like I was missing out, but also that I was being selfish for feeling this way. Some women put up with their husbands staying out drinking at pubs. Some men went every night of the week. My self-doubt was seeping in.

I sat at my desk looking at my computer. The office staff behind me were chatting and drinking. I looked at my inbox one last time before I closed my emails. I looked at the time on my screen. 5 o'clock. I sighed. I was bored. I didn't want to go home and eat pizza alone.

I could go and grab a bite to eat across the road, I thought to myself. I sat there procrastinating. I opened up a new email and started to compose a message.

"Hello, Dimitri…"

What was I thinking, I had discussed this with Dina long ago, I had decided I wasn't going to open that door, was I making a mistake? I wasn't sleeping with the guy so what harm was there in sending a simple email? I hit send.

I began to justify my decision by reminding myself of all the negative aspects of my relationship with Dave. By the time I had finished having a conversation with myself, I was proudly sitting at my desk patting myself on the back. I shut my computer down and I was packing my bag. I began to feel good.

"Emmie, come have a drink with us before you go home," my colleagues called out.

I walked up to them and poured myself half a glass of wine. I was chatting to them and recalling the week. I heard my phone ping and I took it out of my bag. Maybe Dave had finally remembered the date? I looked and it was an email. It was from Dimitri. I wasn't sure I was ready to open it. I was reaffirming to myself I hadn't done anything wrong, but why was I feeling so guilty? I slowly sipped on my wine.

The conversations amongst the staff around me were going straight over the top of my head. I wasn't good at pretending to be social. I hadn't really acquired that skill yet. I excused myself and went back to my desk. I sat back down and read my email on my phone.

Dimitri's email sounded excited. He had exclamation marks all over the place and I quietly laughed to myself. He was never good at hiding his excitement or at grammar. He offered to meet up for yiros.

I replied, "Yes."

What's acceptable in a relationship and what's not? Was catching up with an old friend acceptable? I wondered. Were Dave's drinking habits acceptable? I didn't think so.

I sat at my desk and I began to think of my life and when I married. I accepted the plastic coverings over my dining room table to protect the crochet tablecloth my mother insisted I display. I accepted my mother's suggestions and traditions including her home remedies and instilling fear of the bad in me. No wonder I felt guilty doing something out of the ordinary. Heaven forbid I actually did something that made me happy for once. I was more than just a housewife and a mother. I was an individual who had to fight to forge my own path in life, sifting through the crap of my upbringing. My parents never allowed me the opportunity to develop my own beliefs, I was force fed theirs.

I thought of Rosie and how she would perceive my decision to contact Dimitri. She understood and was supportive of me. She was one of a selected few who knew the truth about my relationship with Dave. Sharni also knew. She wasn't at work otherwise I would have run my haste decision by her first. I would have welcomed her advice. We'd dissect all the pros and cons of a simple catch up with an old mate. She'd probably tell me boredom makes people do crazy shit and I should find other ways to occupy my time.

It's too late, I thought. Who cares anyway? I had to stop doing this. I had to stop punishing myself.

Deep down, I cared. If I really didn't care, my mind wouldn't be so consumed with guilt. My decision should feel right at the time.

I gathered my belongings and said goodbye. I walked to the edge of the pavement and I hailed a taxi driving in my direction. It stopped. Once I was seated in the back, I quickly applied my lipstick and did a final check over in my compact mirror.

The taxi pulled up outside the take-away shop. I got out and made my way inside. Sitting in the corner was Dimitri and two white bags on the table. He had a yiros waiting for me. He looked up and smiled at me. He looked so happy to see me. I sat down a little flustered. He leant over the table and gently brushed away my fringe that had fallen over my face.

"Ella," he smiled.

I caught a whiff of his scent. He still smelt the same from years ago. The same aftershave, the same dress sense, the same sex appeal.

By the time I arrived home Dave was fast asleep. I hadn't realised it was midnight. I wasn't even tired. I was still on a high from seeing Dimitri after all those years. I knew I wouldn't be able to sleep just yet. I made myself a cup of chamomile tea. I sat down on the kitchen stool deep in thought. I thought of my mother and how she would pick chamomile flowers straight from the garden to make my tea as a child. Here I was happily sticking a bag in a cup of boiling water. I began to think of how my life had been conditioned to what my parents thought was best. I wondered what my mother would think if she knew I was out until midnight with another man, a Greek man. My father would probably drop dead on the spot. They would have thought my catch up with Dimitri as a very bad decision. Probably one that would see me sent straight to the gates of Hell. My mother would go on about it and question what if someone had seen me or what would people think? Fuck other people! I deserved a little bit of excitement now and then. I deserved to feel desired again. I deserved Greek take-away.

I chuckled to myself. I finished my tea and made my way to bed. I was happy. I felt good about myself, doing something 'bad' in my life.

"Happy anniversary Em," I whispered.

CHAPTER 16

STRIKE 1

WORKING FULLTIME HAD its challenges. I remembered as a child my mother would get up early to start her day before she left for work. At the crack of dawn, she'd be preparing lunches in the kitchen. By the time I had woken, breakfast would already be spread out on the table ready to eat.

When my father wasn't home, she'd try new food ideas more in line with English cuisine than Italian. I couldn't eat the grapefruit she'd diligently prepare the night before, sprinkled with brown sugar and a horrible fake cherry on top. I preferred scrambled eggs and sausages. Looking back now, maybe she was trying to fit into the common culture as well, better known as the melting pot.

I wasn't as industrious as my mother when it came to keeping her shit together. If I wasn't coping, those around me would know. I relied heavily on yellow post it notes. I had them stuck nearly everywhere, a trail to remind me what I needed to achieve in a day and where I needed to be at any given time.

I would jump up and down if one went missing. It would put my whole day out of sync. It reminded me of the crumb trail left behind by Hansel and Gretel. I'd be lost without them.

When Chloe and XJ were little, they played a trick on me and rewrote my notes. They laid them out in the exact same spots. I flew into the kitchen, late for work, grabbed them all and shoved them into my bag. I went into a meeting, pulled them out and saw they had written how much they loved me. They had written down all the things they wanted to do together with me on the weekend. I had to excuse myself from the meeting. I had realised that day, my kids were my world, my sanity and my purpose.

I had suggestions from others to use my phone to record notes, but they would get the same death stare my father used on me as a child. My system worked for me and my days generally ran smoothly. I wasn't good at asking for help. I preferred to do things myself as to not put anyone else out. Or perhaps knowing it was just easier not to bother.

As I began to work longer hours, I tried to ask my family for help. They were all too busy, so I introduced a new system. I went out and purchased a white board. I had our names and chores drawn up like I would at work, a rostered system that lasted one week in our home. One morning I woke to find the white board had disappeared. When I went looking, I found it in hidden in the tool shed. Someone had written on it with a red marker, "This sucks."

"Dave, can you please cook dinner tonight?" I asked, as I called from work.

I had to stay back for a meeting.

"But I've been working all day," was his response.

I hung up.

Why were women placed under so much pressure? Motherhood had given me a greater degree of empathy. I couldn't explain it, but once I had my children I decided I wanted to help others as well. Motherhood gave me a better understanding of survival. It became my best juggling act.

I was exhausted most days and if it wasn't for my exceptional organisational skills, I'd be lost. There were days I was juggling more than I could handle. Timelines had to be met and demands were being placed upon me wherever I turned. I began to feel like a lynchpin in a thankless job.

Women wanted it all, and in the process were burning themselves to the ground. It seemed that the pendulum of power was compulsively stuck in numerous generations. Society had to amend provisions to allow a better understanding with what women needed. Work-life balance was one of them. I wanted to unlock the way for women so they were given opportunities they deserved. I wanted the momentum to become fashionable for our era and generation.

My mother's generation was reliant on their husbands for decision making. She was smart enough to hold the balance of power when it came to the finances and getting what she wanted. The men were the head of the house. Not in my mother's case.

I knew a woman once who had lost all self-control of her life because of her husband. He professed an undying love and made empty promises for years. She bought what he fed her. In the process she lost all self-esteem to want to develop into anything more than a housewife. Her husband had manipulated her into believing there was nothing more she could achieve in her life. They became co-dependent and she had lost all sense of direction, instead opting to spend her days whining on the phone to others. There's nothing wrong with how some choose to live, but not if they're going to constantly complain and ask "what-if."

I certainly wasn't a pushover and Dave accepted and liked this. He thrived on the fact I worked. He liked that I had my own way of thinking. I wasn't a needy, submissive, desperate individual.

I was fortunate enough to assist women in my role at work who were from diverse cultural backgrounds. I felt blessed to be the one they were sharing their stories of hardship with. I would think of my mother and how hard it must have been for her to come to a foreign country alone without any family. She came to seek opportunities and a better life. It made me appreciate her even more. She had it hard. She only had my father to rely on. She had to learn how to speak a foreign language and assimilate to her surroundings. She had to abide by different rules. She had to learn how to commute and there weren't any donkeys in the suburbs.

"What's for dinner tonight ma?" Chloe asked.

"Pizza," I said.

"What again! This is the third time this week we're eating take-away," she said.

"Well, unless someone else is prepared to cook, it's take-away. That's the best I can do. In fact, that's the only thing I'm prepared to do. I have to watch a political debate tonight and write up my opinion on it. I'm already tired from working all day," I said.

"Why can't you take up knitting, or something else, instead of politics? Why can't you have a different hobby?" Chloe asked.

I looked at Chloe stunned.

"This isn't a hobby, it's a part of my job. I'm leading the way for future generations of women. Imagine how you'd feel if you had the exact same job as your brother and he was being paid more than you simply because he's male! Think about that. Think about how you'd feel if you couldn't access birth control and you were popping out kids every few years. Think about sitting at home because you've lost your job due to pregnancy," I scolded.

"If I were you, I would eat what I got, because I'm ready to go out on strike! I feel like jumping on a plane and flying away! I'm tired and I'm sick of coming home and yelling just so people listen. I'm not the only one who lives in this house. I put food on the table, pay the bills, work, grocery shop, just to mention a few. No one takes into consideration what I do around here until it's not done. I do it anyway until the needs of others are met."

"Start with picking up after yourselves and helping around home. If you're old enough to date, then you're old enough to cook a meal! And that goes for your brother too," I snapped.

"The problem these days is you have everything at your fingertips. You don't have to work hard at anything. If I wanted an answer to a solution I had to walk to the local library and flick through endless encyclopedia's, but you wouldn't even know what they are. If I couldn't spell a word I had to pull out a dictionary. Your generation pulls out a phone," I said.

"My shortcut these days is take-away for dinner, deal with it."

I saw Chloe thinking for a moment. She was raised watching me work and fight for social justice. This wasn't anything new. Both my children knew nothing different than their mother who worked fulltime. Sometimes I was jealous Dave got to spend more time with them when they were little than I did. He'd get to do the fun things like taking them to the movies or letting them stay up late and eating ice-cream together. At times I thought Chloe was resentful of me because of my work demands. I was unable to pick her up from school like the other mothers did. She asked me once why I couldn't be a different mum, not realising I was already trying to be the best mum for her.

"What time is the debate on? I'll watch it with you. I appreciate what you do ma, I'm sorry if I upset you," she said.

Chloe stood up and left the room. When she came back she had the white board and put it back in the kitchen. She took out a bright red marker and ruler. She began to draw up a roster. She looked at me and smiled.

"You've always taught me power in numbers, I guess if we both put our heads together the boys will follow. We should all be chipping in and helping one another," she said.

"Yes, we should have tried this long ago," I replied, smiling.

CHAPTER 17

WHEN THE COOKIE CRUMBLES

I REMEMBERED WHEN I was a little girl, my outings involved spending lots of time at Rosie's house. My parents would visit each Sunday afternoon. I would eagerly wait each week knowing I had something to look forward to. Her mother would always make the best Italian biscotti and desserts. She was an exceptional baker. You could smell the aroma walking up the driveway. She would bake all our special occasion cakes.

One day she decided to make a Greek biscuit called kourabiethes. These were shaped like a little croissant and rolled in icing sugar. They were simply delicious. I recalled the time when I was eating my way through a few and I sneezed because of the powdery sugar. At the same time I inhaled more, causing me to cough hard. The biscuit was dry and the icing sugar plentiful. My mother thought I was choking and hit me hard on my upper back. I ended up vomiting. My father scolded me and told me, "That's what you get for eating Greek food."

XJ's favourite cookies were my homemade chocolate chip variety. He had his own special cookie jar. Abundant with moist, soft, sugar free biscuits. Sometimes I would see Dave sneak a few from the jar. Although he proclaimed he didn't eat biscuits, mine were obviously too tempting to turn down. I would bake only the best batch and when I didn't, they went straight in the bin.

Life with Dave could best be compared to a cookie. We had good batches and bad. We were experiencing worse lately. Dave started to drink heavily mainly because he couldn't process everyday issues like our finances. There never seemed to be enough for him. He always wanted more. More for our future, more for the just-in-case moments and more for his superannuation fund. He was chasing his tail and failing to live in the moment. Money consumed him.

I had found ways around dealing with my stresses, confiding in a selected few of my friends. My walks with Dina were my sanity.

"Dina, Dave and I have decided to separate. I can't afford to rent elsewhere so we have decided to live in separate parts of the house for the time being. We stopped sleeping together months ago. His drinking is the driving force behind my decision. He doesn't recognise he has a problem and prefers to bury his head in the sand. He uses avoidance not to deal with issues."

"I'm glad you've finally made the decision to take a break from your relationship with Dave. You both need space. He needs to sort himself out and so do you. You have been the driving force behind your relationship for years. Maybe time apart to seek clarity is what you both need," Dina said.

"I don't understand why I care so much though. I genuinely don't understand any of this," I said. "I still do things for him, I still try to help him out by cooking and cleaning, but it still goes unnoticed. Some women would have left years ago," I said.

"Do you think Dave can't survive without you? Maybe let him and see what happens. Work on just the relationship you two are supposed to be repairing and stop stressing over cleaning the house and picking up after him. Try to find that middle ground that you both once shared. But if you keep picking up after him you won't. You're living in your own area, stop caring about his. You're also supposed to be living your life too. If you go into his area of the house treat it as you're a visitor and leave everything else alone. There's never going to be change if you keep fixing his shit. Just remember you guys are separated," she said.

We kept walking and the night air was cool brushing up against my warm face. I was deep in thought.

"You're right you know, I'm still being a people pleaser. I'm still worried about what I have to cook for dinner and making sure the kids have enough to eat. When I do cook, they all go out anyway and I'm left there sitting on my own," I said.

"Of course, it's more about your kids and worrying about them, but you then figure that you'd better do the right thing by him too. But they're his kids too and they're grown-ups so they should be able to do things for themselves. Dave's attitude won't change towards you until you give him a reason for it to," she said.

"What do you mean?" I asked her.

"Dave just assumes you will take care of everything as you've always done no matter if you live there or not. He goes away on his golfing trips. You clean the house and look after the kids, cook, and shop for groceries, because he knows you will do it all! You go to his section of the home and complain like you always do, so you correct it and he gets away with it as he always has. If the house is gross and he wants you to clean it tell him to shove it. Let him fix his issues. I'll keep reminding you Em, until it sinks in, you don't owe him. You don't even live there half the time," she said.

"I get what you're saying, but I still keep repeating the same shit over and over again," I said.

"It's because you care Em. It's what was expected of a good girl and a good wife. You look after your family first. What you want isn't important," she said.

I burst out crying. Like a tidal-wave that had come over me, my tears hit. Dina had hit the nail on the head and listening to her words was hard to hear. We stopped walking and she dug deep into her pocket of her grey hoodie and handed me a tissue.

"It's clean," she said.

I took it with a half-smile, blowing my nose. I wiped my tears with the sleeve of my top. Dina touched my arm gently.

"Em, you were the one who told me that it was the expectation, the culture. It's been etched into your psyche from the day you were born. If you had seen another dimension to your mother when you lived at home don't you think you would have been different?" she asked.

I began to think of my upbringing, my fight for my freedom back then and now as an adult I was still fighting. I thought about how unwell I felt and how tired I was beginning to look. My parents were off travelling enjoying their lives and I was still mired down. I felt like I had nothing to look forward to other than my occasional catch up with my friends. I hadn't envisaged or factored separation in my early forties.

"If your mum had said to you, Emanuela, get a life that's your own. Don't stress about having children and a husband, don't stress about giving me grandchildren, do whatever makes you happy. Don't you think you would have been a very different person?" Dina asked.

I was crying so hard now that my tissue evaporated into thin air. I was now relying on the sleeves of my top. Deep within me the sobs surfaced, the trails of teardrops lining the black cotton fabric of my arms. I saw a man come out from his garage and attach a hose to his tap to start watering his front lawn, briefly looking up at us, he continued to water.

"Em, you know I love you and it kills me to see you this way. If I could take away your pain, I would. I'm telling you this because you need to hear it. Start with the word 'NO' and STOP feeling guilty about saying it. It's not fair for him to demand that he comes first. Dave's always been first. If our kids behaved like that, we'd have slapped them upside the head. Well, time to slap Dave upside his head and tell him to shut the fuck up. How does that sound?" she said with her hands up in the air.

"Who keeps leaving the lights on when no one is in the room?" I yelled.

Silence, no reply.

I was having a yelling match with myself. I stomped around the house looking for Chloe and XJ. No sign of them. I walked into the dining room and caught a glimpse of them out the window. I saw they were both outside. They were shooting hoops with the basketball. I knocked hard on the dining room window trying to get their attention. They couldn't hear me over the thumping of the basketball and running around.

I annoyingly sighed and walked into the kitchen to start on dinner. I saw a sink full of dishes and rolled my eyes. I was feeling annoyed and frustrated. I began to sort through them when I heard my phone ping. I dried my hands and walked over to the kitchen bench. I opened the message and saw it was from Dimitri.

"Meet me for a drink later Ella," he texted.

I immediately felt adrenaline running through my veins. A cold shot of excitement. I would love nothing more than to walk out on my dutiful commitments at home into the arms of a Greek man holding a shot glass of Ouzo.

Since our reconnection I began to think more about Dimitri and how wrong it felt having dinner with him. Although I justified it by telling myself it was only take-away. I still felt the chemistry between us after all those years. It hadn't left since my early twenties when we were both at night school. I hadn't felt excitement like that in years. But the excitement came at a price. The guilt was consuming me. It was slowly simmering away inside of me. I had to speak to Dina. I texted him back. I couldn't have a drink with him, I had dishes to wash and dinner to prepare. Was this what my life had become, household chores?

"Sorry. Not tonight," I texted.

I went into my bedroom and closed the door behind me. I rang Dina. I slumped myself down on my bed.

"Hey," I heard her say.

"Dina, I need to speak to you. I have to tell you something," I said.

"What is it?"

"I reached out to Dimitri a while back and he replied straight away. We met that night for yiros, at the same take-away shop we used to go to after night school. It felt really wrong, but I was upset. Dave was at the pub as usual and it was our wedding anniversary. He had forgotten. I emailed Dimitri because I didn't want to go home and sit there alone," I said.

"What's the big deal? You met an old friend for dinner. Did you sleep with him? Did you eat yiros in the back of his Ford Falcon? Did you smother him in tzatziki sauce? Did he tantalize you with his worry beads?" she asked sarcastically laughing.

"NO! Stop joking about this. We ate dinner and chatted about life and where we're both at now. He told me about his wife and I filled him in about Dave. We discussed relationship issues and work stuff. We talked about our time back at night school and how far we've come since then."

"So why are you beating yourself up over this? You have guilt issues that you need to process, and not let it consume you. Do you think Dave feels guilty every Friday night when he's drinking at the pub? Do you think the thought crosses his mind that you're home alone? Stop catastrophising this in your mind. You ate yiros, big deal, and if you did sleep with Dimitri and rocked his boat that's no one's business either. Stop running things past people, you have to do what feels right for you. Besides, you wouldn't cope anyway if you had slept with him. Look at the damage you're already doing to yourself over a simple yiros," she said.

We both began to laugh.

"I don't know what to tell you Em. No one can foresee the future, but I personally don't see any harm in your friendship with him. You never know what might happen down the track. He's not a bad guy, he's not nasty, and he's as genuine as they come. If his intentions were anything different, I would have told you years ago. You've kicked the guy to the curb so many times and he's still hanging around. What can I say? I like him, poor bastard," she said.

"I like Dimitri too. I'm pretty sure he knows that. I'm confident the feeling is mutual. I don't have any expectations of him other than our friendship, that's why we work so well together. We have fun and share the same sense of humour. He pushes my buttons and I push his, that's where it stops. I love him, but in a way that's different to the love I have for Dave. Dimitri feels like someone I've known my entire life. Weird hey," I said.

"Em, you two have something special that's always been there. Who knows, but thinking like this will do your head in. Do what feels right to you. Your instincts will lead the way. Listen to your gut. If you choose to meet up again then you decide. You're an adult. If you choose to eat Greek, then you decide. You don't need other people's approval or blessings."

"Thanks, I appreciate your advice. I know Dimitri will always be there for me and vice versa. He's kind of like the Kalamata olives we used to sell at the continental deli, too good to stop at just one," I said.

Dina laughed, "Yeah we'd scoff a few of those down back in the day."

I hung up and dialled Dimitri's number. No answer. I sent him a text message.

"Hey, it was great catching up the other night. I'm here for you if you ever need to offload. I appreciate reconnecting. I know you're here for me too if I ever need you. I appreciate our friendship."

I went back into the kitchen and started stacking the dishwasher. I began to think about what Dina said. I took her advice on board.

I loved Dimitri. No second thoughts about that. I loved him from the moment I saw him and our eyes locked. I could still visualise in my mind exactly what he was wearing the day we met. Baggy denim shorts and a lime green polo. He was wearing red skater shoes with the laces undone. I went up to him and told him he'd trip over. He told me, "It was the fashion." I remembered laughing at him and telling him he'd break his neck. I told him neck braces weren't in fashion. He accused me of giving him the 'evil eye' and how he'd most likely trip, so he bent down and tied them up.

From that day on he had realised I was someone who spoke my mind and it lit something in him.

He had a quirky way about him, trying to be cool, but not quite pulling it off. Maybe it was his insecurities I could see that led me to feel empathy for him. Maybe I was like my father who liked to rescue strays. Either way, Dimitri and I went on to forge mutual chemistry and trust.

I thought about how I was denied the opportunity to meet Greek boys growing up. My father drilled that into me. It was not ever going to happen. Maybe I secretly felt I was now rebelling in some way. The feelings I had for him ran deep just like the electrically conductive biological wires in my brain. I secretly wanted to kiss him. I wanted to do lots of things to him. Was I being tested? Was I being tempted? Perhaps, but like Dina said, you never know what might happen down the track. I was going to run with that.

Living in the same house with Dave was becoming increasingly difficult. I had to keep reminding myself to keep things real. My marriage was real. We had been together for years. I had to keep reminding myself I had to love Dave even on days that I didn't want to because that was unconditional love. I couldn't quit when it no longer became fun, I had to change my way of thinking. But I also had to factor in the feelings I was having and the pressure I was feeling. Keeping things real meant having bad days that led me to becoming depressed. Some days I felt the pressure more than others. We would run into each other around the place. I had to keep the make-believe out. I couldn't let something outside of the box threaten my sense of security. I would eventually have to draw a line in the sand with Dave if things worsened. I would have to move out. I had to keep that real too. But I couldn't shake my feelings either, I secretly wanted Dimitri.

CHAPTER 18

PICTURES AND POSTS

THE EARLY STAGES of any relationship are always exciting. Dave and I didn't have mobile phones or social media in our days of dating. He would leave little notes under the windscreen wipers of my car. I remembered once he covered my car in heart shape notes. His notes were always well worded. His efforts left me smiling for days.

He had invested so much time into getting my attention and showing me how much I was worth. Dave had class and he knew the way to my heart was through my mind. I enjoyed our intellectual conversations. I discovered early on in our relationship he knew exactly how to stimulate my mind. He would challenge my way of thinking. That was my greatest turn on.

Nguyen Xin was a mutual friend I had met through Jess. He worked as a human rights lawyer. He was attractive with very dark, intense eyes and jet-black hair, heavily gelled up higher than it suited him. He wore a spicy aftershave that reminded me of a beef vindaloo, that had seeped through the pores of his skin after eating it the night before.

We were introduced when we were at Jess' place celebrating her birthday. When I first met him, he reminded me a little of Geoff, Jess' husband. A confident man with a charismatic personality. Nguyen had the same look, not overly bearing, but with a twinkle in his eye that I observed from afar. Nguyen seemed shy at first, but when I'd catch him looking at me it seemed like he was trying to work something out in his brain. It felt like he was summing me up.

At times I felt a little awkward around Nguyen. I hadn't really met anyone like him before. He seemed to have secretiveness to him, he became intriguing. Funnily enough we were both at Jess' house once and he came up to me from behind when I was making myself a cup of coffee. He surprised me and I burnt my hand on the stove. I should have taken that as a sign.

Not long after that evening Nguyen sent me a friend request via social media and we became 'real' friends. The concept of this was just as confusing to me as the cultural imbalance I felt at school as a child. I really didn't know where I fitted in. I would see Nguyen out and about, but we never really had meaningful face to face conversations. There was no real connection, other than our mutual friend. But once we became online friends, he was completely different. His conversations were as intense as his personality. This was his avenue where he unleashed his true persona.

Nguyen began to message me daily and called me "beautiful".

I didn't like strangers calling me "darl" or "hon" to my face, but I allowed a complete stranger to refer to me as beautiful. He had an orchestrated way with words.

My newly found friend began to offer me a pleasant distraction from my humdrum life and it felt exhilarating. My confidence grew at work. I was making decisions and showing real leadership. I began to grow as an individual overnight. My self-esteem skyrocketed. I often wondered why I was so lucky that he picked me. Was our meeting a coincidence? At times I would zone out during work meetings and visualise an archery board, and Nguyen shooting an arrow straight into the bullseye. With perfect precision he chose me. But

Nguyen was different to any other man I had met before. His form of communication wasn't the conventional type. I had never experienced sexting before.

He would send me provocative pictures. Electronic devices and technology made it all too easy for him to do so. He wasn't as creative as Dave when he was chasing me. A lot less effort and thought. He seemed experienced in this area and I felt my first ping of self-doubt.

When I received the first photo it was very early on in our relationship and I was shocked and surprised. I hadn't really known him all that long to be receiving those sorts of messages. It left me scratching my head in bewilderment and wondering how I should reply. I didn't know what to make of it, so I politely made something up. I didn't want to hurt his feelings, but it seemed crazy to me. Politeness was about to open up a world of hurt for me.

"Wow!" I texted, and left it at that. More of a shock horror 'wow' than a pleasant one.

That was the best I could come up with at the time. He had caught me off guard.

I wasn't interested in naked photos of him. I never asked for one to be sent. It was more of a turn off than a turn on. He thought he was on a winner, and continued to send them. I preferred to keep my intimate thoughts in the bedroom. I didn't have anything to prove and I wasn't one to seek outside validation so I never sent any back.

Electronic communication became a new avenue for dating and the modern-day hazards that came with it.

It did prompt me into thinking what my father had taught me growing up about class boundaries. He liked Dave because he was from the east side of town, but Dave was also articulate, honourable, and polite. He was respectful towards women and he was a good family man. He was also a good provider. He suited our extended family well and slotted in easily.

Nguyen was from the west side of town. He had an edge to him and he was more of a risk taker and attention seeker. He even dressed differently to Dave. But my father had a prejudicial regional mindset. He liked to help those less fortunate and thought education was the key to unlocking a better future for the social disadvantaged. I guess regional mindsets didn't really determine how people should interact towards one another, rather their values and morals did.

"Dina, what do you think of guys who send nude photos? Especially when they're sent to women they've only just met?" I asked.

"If it's consensual, and you've both agreed to it, then it's okay, but I personally don't like them. I think any man who has to send a naked photo to a love interest is full of himself. He's egotistical. He's seeking attention and most likely lacks self-esteem. Or it could be a way to make them feel empowered. Either way, it's a highly impersonal form of communication. I guess guys who do that could potentially be doing it to many women and you wouldn't be none the wiser. It's already setting up a precedent of their style towards relationships. No time invested or real emotional connection. If I had only just met a guy and he sent me a photo of himself showering or laying naked on his bed, I'd question his integrity. I'd begin to think they obviously like to brag about themselves. Clearly, they need people to look at them. Almost like a peacock. It's like watching birds trying to attract a mate. He does his little dance and flaps his wings and waits for the gullible ones to respond. For me, it's about having pride and wanting to attract the right person. For him, it could be just about attracting attention and taking his pick. Those types of men are not for me," she said.

"Why are you asking?"

"No reason, I was just curious. You know with the social technology hype and the lack of privacy and safety issues these days anything can be shared around," I said.

"It's all too easy nowadays. The dating process like we once knew it has gone out the window," she said.

"It's not only the dating process that's changed, but the way people communicate as well. It's similar to texting and talking. I'd rather pick up the phone and have a conversation than spend five minutes writing up a message and going back and forth," I said.

"I agree. I prefer having conversations and I like to see Darren in real life, face to face. That goes for in the bedroom too, not in some photo. Plus, you can spice up your sex life in other ways. Maybe a little more creative than just firing off a nude photo," she said.

"Yes, Dave and I used to be inventive back in the day. We'd make time for one another. We'd put thought into our time spent alone. We'd have date nights where we'd go out to nice restaurants and then have sexy sleepovers in fancy hotels. I guess we became time poor and with kids coming along, putting effort and creativity into our intimacy took a back seat. We used to go at it like rabbits," I laughed.

"We even went skinny dipping one night. Dave took me to a secluded beach once. It was pitch black and it was a hot summer night. It was really late. We had to walk over sand dunes to get to the beach. Once we got there all we saw were the stars and the water. We stripped and ran in. It was the best night. I miss those days. We had fun back then," I said.

"Times have changed, Em. Sexual-gratification is at your fingertips these days. If a guy thinks a photo of his junk is all the effort required, then he's not normal in the way he thinks relationships should work. Especially if you haven't agreed to it, it makes it even more awkward. It's a shitty way of trying to build a real relationship. Particularly in the early stages of getting to know someone. A confident man wouldn't feel the need to send those sorts of messages. In fact, he wouldn't feel the need to boast about anything. Not how much money he earns, his job status, his accolades. A nice, decent man would have enough sense and confidence to allow him to embrace relationships, not stand and spruik on his podium. If someone sent me a photo like that early on, it would sound alarm bells for me," she said.

I began to think of my days with Dave and how much I missed him. He was familiar and had a set of old fashion values. He challenged me in ways that enabled me to grow and become a better person. Nguyen wasn't someone I was trusting. My conversation with my best friend was only reaffirming what I was already feeling. I wasn't familiar with this form of communication. Dina was right, he was probably sending those sorts of pictures to other women as well. Maybe it was his calling card.

CHAPTER 19

BUYER BEWARE

WHEN I MARRIED Dave, I had envisaged a life-time together where we would eventually be sitting in our golden years on a swinging love seat holding hands. In my mind, I had created the perfect life that bypassed any problems altogether. I failed to factor in growth and change. I thought Dave and I would remain the same two people, who took their wedding vowels, for better or for worse, till death do us part. Life doesn't work that way. Marriage was not my magic cure to make problems disappear. I hadn't factored in that we would change.

I couldn't predict my future. Italians believed in superstition and signs from above. Maybe Nguyen was a sign. If I had taken the time to observe, I too would have seen the signs. I would have seen big bright red fucking flags. Eleven of them lined up in a row. Ten wouldn't have been enough. I always needed the extra push when it came to recognising signs and avoiding danger. I was the type of person who needed the extra kick while I was down. Or like Dina would say, "A big fat slap across the face!" To wake me up and see reality for what it really was.

"Emmie, I thought you would appreciate this article I found on volunteering in a soup kitchen for a women's shelter in the city. I'll send you the link," Nguyen text messaged late one night.

"Hey there, thank you I really appreciate that," I replied.

"We could help out together if you'd be interested. I wouldn't mind doing something like this," he texted.

"I'd like that," I replied.

"Why don't we meet up for a drink to discuss this?" he texted.

"Sure, why not," I replied.

I was surprised Nguyen found an interest in me. I was surprised he wanted to be a part of my life. I was surprised he wanted to do volunteer work with me. I had surprises all around me that generally came late at night through a text message. I couldn't stand anyone else texting late at night, but I felt the need to be polite and reply. I didn't want to come across as rude to my 'new friend'.

I had boundaries with my other friends and texting late at night was no go. Unless they had been captured by the mafia and held hostage for my secret ricotta balls in sauce recipe. Then I might reconsider.

To the outside world I was a mother and a wife who juggled full-time work. That was my role and my comfort zone. I wasn't someone to share my dirty laundry. Maybe this guy had superpowers, maybe he could see deep into my soul that I was actually searching for something more. I had been searching my entire life, and this made me sad. I still thought I hadn't achieved greatness. The only problem was, I didn't know if I'd recognise it once I found it.

I was looking to find my place in society and in this world. I didn't know how and I didn't care, but I was rolling with it. I wanted to forge a path for others to follow. I was a leader and a mentor.

Nguyen's work involved interstate travel. He mentioned how he would like me to go with him some time. I figured I could? Dave and I were sleeping in separate rooms and things weren't great between us. We hardly saw one another.

We were playing a game of pretend to our friends and family. Not on-line, but rather to their faces. We wanted our children to have a stable home environment, regardless if we were speaking to one another or not.

My friendship with Nguyen progressed pretty quickly. In fact, it was moving at a pace best described like if I were at an all you can eat dessert buffet. I'd scoff down as much as I could and as quickly as possible because my eyes were bigger than my stomach. I'd want to try all the variety on offer. Before I knew it, I'd feel like throwing up from overindulging.

His words would make my head spin. No sooner would he say the most enchanting things, I would be swept off my feet. Our friendship was quickly reclassified and jumped the queue and became a relationship. And there was a big difference between the two.

"You've got me, Emmie. I'm all yours," Nguyen said after our first kiss.

"You're incredible, Emmie. I can't wait to make love to you. Trust me Emmie, I know what's best for you," he said.

I did trust Nguyen, I had no reason not to. That's what people in relationships do, trust and respect one another. He was an articulate individual that won legal battles for refugees to remain in Australia. He was always well planned and strategically organised. He knew exactly how to win. He had won me over. I was honest with him and I had nothing to hide. I was open and transparent. I shared my vulnerabilities with him. In fact I had served them up on a silver platter.

"Emmie, come away with me for the weekend to my cabin by the beach. We can spend some time there and we can pretend we're invisible. No one will be there, all the neighbours are away," he said, when he called me.

"Sure, I'd like that. I'd like to be anonymous for once," I happily said.

Nguyen's cabin was simple, it smelt a little musty. Nothing too fancy, but it made do for his getaways when life became a little too much for him. He once told me it was the perfect location to spend alone time. He said he liked to reflect and meditate. He practiced mindfulness.

It was directly opposite a secluded beach. The view was incredible. It was where the ocean met the white sand underneath the vast bright blue sky. It was an uninhabited little piece of paradise. Casting my eyes and looking to one side I saw there were jagged rocks on a cliff face that met the ocean. I was at peace with nature.

Our long quiet walks along the beach weren't hand in hand. Nguyen preferred to walk alone with me in tow behind him. He always seemed so deep in thought. I tried talking to him, but it seemed more of an annoyance than a welcomed conversation. I didn't mind, I accepted him as he was. He was a man of very few words. His eyes were as intense as his moods. One minute he was kissing me, the next he would offer me a glass of red wine. I obligingly drank it.

He had lots of wine in his cabin. I was surprised because he made a point of stopping along the way to buy more bottles for our overnight stay. He said it was so we could relax and unwind together. I didn't need alcohol to unwind. I welcomed conversations and getting to know one another better.

"Emmie, come sit by me. Let's have a wine together," he said handing me a glass.

I stood up from the front steps of the cabin and sat next to him on the cane chair on his verandah. The little sea ornaments hanging by the front door reminded me of a cabin in the Hamptons. Whitewashed walls with blue star fish tacked to the cladding. The cane chairs we were sitting on were an oak-grey colour well-worn from the sea mist.

"Talk to me Nguyen, tell me about your life," I suggested.

"So, you want me to talk to you?" he asked.

I was confused, was I supposed to just sit in silence drinking? This wasn't my idea of a little getaway, I was beginning to feel bored. I could spend alone time in the comfort of my own home, not like a ghost drinking on someone's deck.

"Yes, you can talk to me about anything," I said excitedly.

"You're better off without me, you can do so much better than me. I'm not the person who you think I am. The grass isn't greener on the other side," he said.

"What do you mean?" I asked.

I was surprised. He became very defensive. This was not a normal sort of conversation I had in mind. I wanted to share stories about everyday life and work, his upbringing, his friends. All of a sudden, our conversation had taken a turn down the road of dark self-pity.

"Emmie, you're still living under the same roof as Dave. Maybe if you left your situation behind it will give me a chance to be with you or it will give you a chance to discover who you really are. You're a sophisticated, classy lady, but you need to do what's right for you," he said.

He stood up and took out another bottle of red wine sitting in a box by the front door. He opened the bottle and poured himself another glass.

His jeans looked worn and his black top looked like it went through the whites only cycle.

"I don't like drama, Emmie. I like the simple life, I'm happy to live life on my own. I could live out of a caravan if I had to. I don't need the modern commodities to get by. Women these days are too consumed by first world problems, they're too much into their image," he said.

"They have to have thousand-dollar handbags to feel good about themselves."

My anger began to rise within me, my face began to look and feel like his glass of Shiraz, red hot. I tried to keep calm, but the fact he stereotyped women made me seethe. I took a deep breath.

I thought of the conversations Dave and I shared and they were more normal and less dry than this type. There would be no mention of first, second or third world problems. If we encountered problems, we would sort them out together and place importance on them. We would work as a team to resolve issues, not categorise them. Dave certainly wasn't sexist, he supported women.

My stomach began to feel uneasy and I wasn't feeling well. Perhaps I drank too much wine or perhaps this guy was starting to show signs of how complex he really was. He knew my circumstances. This hadn't stopped him from asking me away for the weekend together. Last week Nguyen idolised me. My confusion was beginning to get the better of me.

"Nguyen, I'm sorry you feel this way about women. I disagree. Maybe past experiences have led you to think this way. I'm not like that," I said.

Before I could continue my conversation, I saw someone walking up the beach. As she approached us, I could see her long blonde hair bouncing in the breeze. Nguyen stood up and waved, with his hand high above his head he caught her attention and she waved back. Excitedly she ran towards us. She was thin, wearing tiny shorts and a cotton singlet, making her big breasts look even bigger, hugging her figure.

"Hi Nguyen!" she said excitedly.

"Hi Liz! I didn't think anyone was down here this weekend?" he asked her.

They continued to chat, Nguyen running his fingers through his jet-black hair. He casually stood leaning up against a porch post. Liz was smiling her perfectly straight, pearly-white teeth.

I stood up and walked over to them. Nguyen's body language had changed, and he looked so much more receptive and excited standing opposite Liz. I could smell sex appeal oozing from his pores. They were happily chatting and I felt like I was interrupting them with my presence. Were these my insecurities surfacing or were these my instincts telling me this wasn't a simple neighbourly chat? I was beginning to feel like the third wheel. I was standing by his side for what began to feel like forever, time embarrassingly ticking by. I was yet to be introduced and I was feeling awkward.

"Liz, this is Emmie," he said tilting his head towards me.

"Pleased to meet you," I extended my hand to shake hers.

"Oh? I better be off then," she said with a smirk.

She looked at me a little awkwardly. It felt antagonising. She looked back at Nguyen with a stupid smile, flicking her long blonde hair as she took off up the beach.

"Bye, Lizzie," he said beaming.

I looked at Nguyen and I saw a twinkle in his eye. It was the same look I saw when we first met.

"Lizzie is someone who shares the same interests as me. She's very intelligent. She is bubbly and fun to be around, everyone likes her. Maybe you could get to know her a little better, you should send her a friend request. You could learn a thing or two from her," Nguyen said.

This wasn't the first time Nguyen made comparisons between me and other women. I knew all about his past lovers and the similarities we supposedly shared. He seemed to always be looking back into his past, where I preferred to be present in the moment. If someone is 'into you' they don't make comparisons with others to fuel insecurities or plant the seed of doubt.

Nguyen was beginning to remind me of my swimming. I liked to remain between the two red flags the lifesavers put out as a safety precaution. I could see at that very moment my first red flag with Nguyen, he preferred to swim outside of these. He was still watching Liz make her way home, captivated by their brief encounter.

CHAPTER 20

STRIKE 2

DAVE'S BELOVED MOTHER Tillie had passed away peacefully. Loss and heartache fixed in his heart and brain, every fibre of his being hurting. She was a beautiful soul, hardworking and task driven. Chloe looked up to her as her mentor and her woman in leadership. She was fiercely strong minded and spoke the truth. She called it like it was. She fought hard right up until the end. She didn't want to leave, but she left with words of wisdom etched in all our minds. We missed her so much. She was surrounded by her family holding her hands as she left to take her forever journey.

Grief and loss hurt. The way people dealt with it was differing. Some chose to talk about it and others were best left alone. My journey of grief was to make it easier for those around me and I didn't have time to mourn. I was too busy taking care of the needs of others. I missed Nanna Smith too. I secretly cried, but I couldn't focus on my healing because I was about to step into an entirely different sort of relationship. Dave wasn't dealing well with his grief. He decided to block it all out. With twelve bottles of beer each day, Dave had discovered benders.

Addictions are an intriguing thing. I was addicted to nail biting as a child. I was so addicted I didn't have a problem eating away at myself. It became a dirty habit. My parents tried everything from hot chilli powder to rubbing soap on them. It was only until one day I gnawed so much that my fingers began to bleed and the light bulb switched on in my mind. I was actually eating my DNA, gross! So, I stopped.

My father was addicted to cigarettes. It was all the rage in the '70s and '80s until the medical profession decided to campaign for change and introduced the 'C' word, cancer. My father stopped smoking. Cold turkey, no questions asked. Not because he was afraid of dying, but because my mother told him she refused to take care of him if he became unwell. She'd put him in a nursing home instead. He said the food in those places was terrible and that thought alone was enough for him to quit.

We all loved Nanna Smith, but she shouldn't be remembered through an addiction. She would have been turning in her grave if she saw the way Dave was behaving. She would have slapped him upside his head and told him in no uncertain terms to get his shit together! She loved her son as she loved all of her boys. Dave's brothers were dealing with loss in different ways. I was supporting the lot of them. I didn't have time to grieve. I had others to take care of.

Celebrations were always hard. Missing loved ones, who were once there to join in the festivities. Dave struggled with most family events, preferring to stay home drinking instead. His grief seemed selfish to me because he had children and me who missed his mother just as much as he did.

I always made a point of remembering the dearly departed. Unlike my culture, I chose not to wear black during a period of mourning. Instead I would honour their memory by planting a special tree or plant, connecting with nature instead. This was my holistic approach to death.

Nanna Smith loved tulips, so Chloe and I planted bulbs all around the edging of an old gum tree in the backyard. We decorated the tree with solar love heart shaped fairy lights and plastic butterflies hanging from its branches. We even planted some in a special pot and put them by her grave site. Chloe hand painted the pot, adding her special touch.

As the months passed Dave's grief darkened. I tried my best to help him, but I became the enemy. I retreated and left him alone. His grief became a habitual excuse to not address his issues. His grief was masking a deep psychological scar and it was sending him spiralling out of control.

I went and sought counselling and I was told grief was high up on the ladder of stress causing depression, as was relationship break-ups and moving to a new house. I was dealing with all three. Dave just didn't know it yet. Depression hit both of us. We just made our acquaintance at different stages. Dave met depression through grief.

"Pleased to meet you," I'm sure it said to his brain, then wiring up the connectors to make a home. It became a squatter and hard to evict.

I met depression when Dave and I began to argue. He was a lonely figure who had convinced me the deeper I sank into my dark hole that no one would find me. He tricked me under the guise of offering solitude and safety.

Our behaviour towards one another had an impact on all around us. I was trying to convince myself how bad our relationship was so I could justify separation being the best way to move forward. I mean what would people say or think? They loved Dave. He wasn't a bad person, he was troubled.

Dave was a highly intelligent man. He was revolutionary in his thinking. He was the type of guy that would look at the whole picture. He never gave too much away. I found it hard helping him when he didn't share what he had locked up in his brain. I wasn't a mind reader. I knew he was struggling, we all did. He lost weight and wasn't sleeping. He wasn't moody like other alcoholics, but he did throw tantrums now and then. I began to think Dave was stuck in grief unable to move forward.

"The way that you're behaving isn't going to bring back your mother," I said.

"Don't mention her, I don't want to think about it now," was his response.

"I think I should move out for a short time," I said. "I think we need space."

"Great, so I have to deal with this too, my support is leaving me. I'll have no one. Thanks a lot Emmie!" he shouted.

"That's the problem Dave, I actually don't know how to support you. This is driving me around the twist. I don't know what I'm coming home to each night when I walk through the front door. I feel anxious and uncertain about my own mental health and my life," I said.

"Welcome to my world!" he said.

"Dave it's been nearly three years since your mother has passed away. She wouldn't want to see you like this! I feel like I'm getting stress ulcers. I'm not going to put my health on the line and stick around until you decide you want to get your shit together," I said.

"Our family life has become dysfunctional. The kids are never home. I don't want to be at home. You're off on benders. You say the most horrible things to me and then expect forgiveness. I can't keep up anymore. I feel like I'm suffocating here," I said.

"Do what you need to do then, I don't care!" he said.

"I don't care," had become his standard answer to everything.

Dave did care. He cared very much for his family and our relationship, but I couldn't help him if he wasn't prepared to help himself.

I remembered my conversations I'd have with my mother-in-law. She would tell me if you really loved someone and they couldn't be helped, then you had to walk away. It was called tough-love. It was a way of shocking them and prompting them to find the means to help themselves. I just didn't know there would come a day that I had to exercise this same practice on her son. I was left with no choice. I couldn't deal with Dave anymore and stay sane at the same time. I felt like I was already crazy.

Packing and moving out was hard. Dave was so angry he kicked a cardboard box I had packed and put to one side. I didn't react. I just waited until he left and repacked it. I booked the removalist to arrive when he was at work. I had my leave at work planned and booked to allow me time to unpack and settle into my rental. It took me nearly a week to finally move out. And when I had, I realised I could breathe again. I needed space in order to find clarity.

I didn't hate Dave, in fact the opposite, I loved him.

"Emmie, I miss you," he texted me one night.

"Same," I wrote back.

CHAPTER 21

CHINESE TAKE-AWAY

How do things go from bad to worse so fast? My relationship with Dave seemed like it disintegrated overnight. I didn't even remember how it all happened. It was like a whirlwind that spiralled out of control. But when it did, deep down I was happy it had hit an all-time low. Because once you hit rock bottom, there's only one way out and that's up. That was Dave's all-time low. I didn't know I was yet to experience mine. I thought I had my shit together.

I felt like someone had given me the 'evil eye' and I needed my mother to pull out the bowl of water and olive oil. But there wasn't enough salt in the world to make my evil eye disappear. I would have to start walking around with cloves of garlic in my pockets to ward of what was about to hit me right in my face.

Dave was moving forward. He was seeking help. He was fighting for himself and for me. He refused to see a future without me. I was the love of his life and it felt strange knowing this. It reminded me of what my mother had once told me about him. She said he was a decent man because he would always fight to have me in his life. He wasn't someone who ran away. I guess she was right. She could see something in him that I couldn't at the time. I was young and too busy romanticising my life and making up stories in my head.

My relationship with Nguyen progressed as quickly as my other one deteriorated. He swooped in on me like a magpie attacking a bike rider sending her flying over the handlebars.

I never really saw it coming and I never saw the damage it could do.

He would entice me over to his place with his home cooked meals, proclaiming he made everything from scratch. He liked to compare himself to famous Asian chefs by watching their cooking shows on television.

"I'm going to open up my own café one day," he said.

"I'm sick of dealing with legal issues and stupid people, I want to cook instead."

Nguyen was a good cook, but doesn't everything taste better when someone else prepares it after a long day? There weren't too many things I didn't eat that he prepared. He did cook a good steak, but you had to eat it his way. Otherwise you were called 'stupid' for not attempting to taste the semi-live gourmet version he'd prepare. No choices there either. Something I was accustomed to growing up.

He made a great hollandaise sauce, and slapped it all over Atlantic salmon, but he had lots of packets stashed in the back of his pantry cupboard.

He told me he made the best pizza dough. I went and opened his freezer once and was faced with boxes of frozen pizzas, the variety found at the supermarket. Perhaps these were signs too. I'd make my selection and throw it in the oven. Beggars can't be choosers when you're hungry late at night.

He made fried rice once, then I found the plastic take-away containers in the bin. It still tasted okay. I feigned my thanks and appreciation for him preparing dinner that evening. He would often tell me he was feeding me one thing, but I'd end up eating something entirely different.

My highs and lows were now shared with him. At least with Dave I could work around our issues, because we knew one another so well. I already knew what I was getting with him. We were like comfort food on a cold winter evening. No preservatives, just wholesome saucy nourishment.

I didn't like how Nguyen made me feel at times, but I kept going back for more. *Why?* I'd often ask myself. Had I become addicted to making up and breaking up? Or was it that I was his side dish? I was an intelligent level-headed individual and I was caught up in a whirlwind of senseless, timewasting emotions. At the time I was convinced I deserved Nguyen. He showered me with all the 'right' attention. A very unrealistic version. I would brush his inappropriateness to one side and forgiveness stepped in.

I was once described by a colleague as a driven, determined, confident individual when I was thanked for my contribution to community involvement with local gardens. But now I was best described as Scarlett O'Hara from *Gone with the Wind*, except I wasn't a closet alcoholic. She too was chasing her tail and ended up losing the person she loved the most. The one person who stood right in front of her.

My heart was still torn between looking for the normal, and trying to bypass the crazy. My mind didn't know which road to turn down. The mixed messages Nguyen gave me were best described like a bag of mixed salted nuts. Each time I would fish deep in the packet for a cashew I'd end up with the Brazil nut. The worst one in the entire pack. The nut no one ate because of its woody texture and horrible bitter after taste. The nut I'd always try to avoid ending up with.

I was looking forward to catching up with Nguyen. I hadn't seen him for a few weeks. He didn't cope well when I was stressed about issues outside of our relationship. He preferred to see me when I was calm and worry-free. It was interesting he perceived me as stressed, trying to convince me I should spend more alone time to deal with my issues. For all I knew, he was finding other ways to entertain himself in between the times he didn't see me. Convincing me to sort my issues out probably suited his schedule. He tried hard to convince me I was 'troubled'.

My job was advocating for others. Failing to see the irony, I should have been advocating for myself, first and foremost. Ditching the Brazil nut wasn't as easy as I had anticipated.

Nguyen said he didn't like drama around him. I didn't like how I couldn't share my day with him without being picked on, criticised or called dramatic. You'd think sharing your day with someone you're sharing your life with was a normal, mature thing.

"Hi! I've missed you!" I said running up to him at the café.

"I've missed you too Em," he said kissing me.

"Let's get a table in the corner," I said, pointing to empty seats.

"I want to tell you all about Jess. She's moved out and she's now renting. She's still struggling a little. I'd like to run past some ideas with you on how I can keep helping her. I want her to be financially secure and not have to worry about money at a time like this. Breakups can be hard when they're not amicable. You've got a good understanding of these sorts of situations. What do you think?" I asked.

"Jess needs to work on herself, she lacks confidence. She's acting like the victim. She'll never pick herself up and you trying to help her will only reinforce her victim mentality," he said abruptly.

"That's harsh, considering it was Geoff who was cheating," I said.

"She is a victim of infidelity. She's trying her best, she relied heavily on Geoff, and she actually loved him and their family unit."

I began to wish our conversations weren't always this intense. Nguyen was someone my high school Principal,

Sister Josephine would best describe as 'Mentem omnia in deterius', a fucking pessimist.

Nguyen looked disinterested in our conversation. He was trying to engage, but his frown spoke louder than his words.

The waitress came over and took our coffee orders and walked away. He watched her walk back to the counter.

"I think she likes me," he said. "I think she'd try and chat me up if you weren't here."

I ignored his comments and pretended to look at the small menu on our table.

The café was quiet, warm and cozy. Nguyen looked handsome, a little tired, but that was nothing new. He was wearing a black coat and black jeans. He reminded me of a ninja warrior, someone you can't hear coming, but deadly enough when you eventually saw him.

He placed his mobile phone on the table. I was surprised because he'd normally keep it in his pocket. He wouldn't use it in front of me. I used to think that was a polite and respectful gesture.

"I've left my wallet in the car, I'll be back in a minute," Nguyen said.

He got up to leave and he left his phone behind. My Italian kicked in, or rather my instincts. I knew I shouldn't invade his privacy, but I felt like some unknown force pushed my hand towards it. I looked up and quickly scanned the room. From where we were sitting, I could see the front entrance to the café. I picked up his phone. It had a pin code. *This is so wrong!* I thought to myself. *Do it!* Another voice said.

I typed in his date of birth. No, declined. I typed in his post code. No, declined. As I went to put the phone down I gave it one last shot.

I could feel my hands starting to become clammy and my heart beating faster. I began to feel dizzy. I typed in the number in the title of his favourite science-fiction movie *2001: A Space Odyssey*. BINGO. I couldn't believe it. I was in, and my heart felt like it was thumping in my head.

I quickly looked at his text messages. My eyes were scanning for anything that would stand out to me. As I scrolled down, I saw 'Lizzie.' I opened it.

The last message he had sent her was the weekend we went away together at his cabin by the beach. It was sent at 1 o'clock in the morning by Nguyen.

"Do you want me to tuck you in?" he had texted her.

I quickly shut the messages and put his phone down on the table exactly where he had left it, as I saw him walking back to the café. I sat there, numb, feeling like I had been roundhouse kicked in the chest, the force knocking the wind out of me.

CHAPTER 22

DINNER'S AT VI O'CLOCK

SOME DIDN'T UNDERSTAND the difference between right and wrong. They weren't raised to identify the difference clearly. Growing up it was pretty straight forward for me. If I did something wrong as a child, my father would take off his leather belt and threaten to hit me. I'd run for cover and never repeat what I had done ever again. Doing the right thing was an expectation, which was easy. For me growing up, life was pretty much black and white. As an adult, I had to learn about boundaries. The grey area.

It felt like I had nailed myself to a wooden cross, I had become an expert at self-punishment. My shoulders would physically hurt from the guilt I was carrying. The pain that I had created in my mind was all self-inflicted. I had created real physical pain, as well as the emotional type. I felt like I deserved to be punished, and what better person to do this but me. I wasn't sleeping or eating. I was consumed by what I had perceived, in my mind, as having done the wrong thing. I wasn't coping.

"Em, are you okay? You don't look too good," Sharni asked me at work.

"Actually, I'm not feeling the best, Sharni. My stomach is killing me, I've done something really bad," I said.

"Like what? Are you in some sort of trouble? Did you get caught poster bombing front doors of political offices again? That's not fair if you've run a campaign without me. I love doing that sort of stuff!" she exclaimed.

"No, it's nothing like that, it's a personal thing," I said.

We were both standing at the photocopier. We had just come out of a meeting and I was finishing up my tasks for the day.

"Em, it's nearly 6 o'clock, let's go get dinner. Tell me what's going on," she suggested.

"Sure, let me finish my printing, I'll meet you across the road," I said.

Sharni gave me a little squeeze of my arm as she walked off to gather her things.

When I arrived the small Thai restaurant seemed surprisingly busy for a Wednesday night. There were people waiting in line to collect take-away by the front counter. The owner had grown to know Sharni and I quite well. Located not far from work, it was a convenient spot to grab a bite to eat when we had to work back. He smiled at me as I entered and tilted his head towards where Sharni was sitting. I saw her sitting in the corner waiting for me. I took my seat opposite her. I was tired and depressed. I slumped into my chair melding into its shape, feeling like Goldilocks when she found the right chair for her.

"What's going on?" she asked.

"It's Nguyen," I said.

"What now?" she asked sounding annoyed.

I felt uneasy repeating the same issues over and over to my best friend. I already had, a hundred times before. The same topics open to discussion with Sharni. There's only so much friends can take of the same old merry-go-round type of crap in one's life. Her advice offered quite often was dissected and analysed in my brain, but rarely acted upon.

Sharni had met Nguyen a few times. She didn't like him and tried to tell me, but I didn't listen.

As my relationship with Dave was depleting, I relied more on Nguyen for support. I thought this was the normal thing to do when two people proclaimed to love one another. You lean on each other for comfort in times of need.

I had only recently moved out of the marital home and was now renting. The move had taken its toll on me. Packing and unpacking, my best friends were better known as a screwdriver and an allen key assembling furniture in-between my other commitments. I'd come home late at night and stay up until the early hours of the morning emptying boxes.

Nguyen hadn't even been around to see my new home yet, making excuses each time I extended an invitation. He told me he had moved homes that many times in his life, he just did what he had to do, and I should stop complaining. I was lucky to have a roof over my head.

"My relationship with him is worse than learning trigonometry. I don't know where to look to find the right solution to make this work and I don't trust him," I said.

"I stupidly checked his phone messages and emails the other night when I went over to his place. He left them open on his laptop and when he was in the shower and I checked them. The guilt is seriously killing me."

"What did you find?" she asked.

I told her about the message I read that he had sent to Liz. I told her how that made me feel, the fact I was asleep in his bed while he was 'tucking' someone else in. I told her how wrong it was of me to play detective, but my stomach was telling me something wasn't right. I went on to explain how I was dousing myself with guilt and ready to set myself alight.

The waitress walked over and took our food order.

"Can you please make my noodles without nuts, I'm allergic," I said.

She nodded and we continued to talk.

"When did you become allergic to nuts?" Sharni asked.

"I haven't been able to stomach them lately, they make me feel unwell. I've developed an intolerance," I said.

"Em, in all the years you've been married to Dave did you once feel the need to check his phone?" she asked.

"No, but what's that got to do with my current situation?" I asked.

"Clearly your instincts are prompting you to play detective because Nguyen isn't making you feel secure. If he was, there would be no need for games. Can't you see the drama that surrounds this guy? He's not genuine at all. There's no trust there. I'm surprised he hasn't developed separation anxiety when he leaves his phone behind," she said.

"Do you remember the time you were distraught, you weren't coping with the move, you had boxes everywhere and the removalists bailed on you. You had your boxes waiting on the front lawn, it took you hours of work to get them out there ready to go. It started to rain and you had to move them all back inside. Later when you messaged Nguyen, you had to pretend everything was okay otherwise he'd think you were being dramatic. He was away overseas and he took his time responding. You got upset and fired off a nasty message?" she asked.

"Yeah, that was my downfall," I replied.

"No way! Instead of saying something like, 'Honey I don't know why you're texting me this, but I'm here for you, I love you', he said, 'Okay, see you later'. There was no fight in his message. Can't you see he's not equipped to be in a normal adult relationship? Normal adults don't tell you you're their soul mate one minute and then the next minute you on longer exist in their lives," she reminded me.

"Sharni there's something else too," I said.

"What?" she asked.

"When Nguyen went overseas, he posted photos on social media. Even though I refuse to be his online friend because of his bullshit make-believe nine hundred plus friends, I could still see his posts. He had them on public, maybe knowing I'd see them or perhaps orchestrating them for me. I noticed one person in particular was commenting continuously. It was Liz. When I checked her profile, she had a partner so I kind of felt safe, but it was a false sense of safe. When I looked closer and dug deeper, she was overseas with Nguyen. They went together," I said sounding disappointed.

"When I look up her then 'partner' he has now changed his status to single. He is gorgeous, look!" I said, as I pulled out my phone and typed his name in the search bar.

Sharni leant over to take a look at my phone.

"Wow, she left him for what reason? For Nguyen? You've got to be kidding me. So, he's ruined another relationship too has he? Automatically thinking he has exclusive rights to another is very self-entitled. Probably spun her the same story he spun you. Smooth words and empty promises," Sharni said.

I sat there feeling defeated. The look on my face spoke a thousand words.

"Sorry Em, I didn't mean it like that, but seriously go get some couples counselling with Dave and fuck this moron off. I'm sorry, I know this must be hard to hear, but as your friend I have to say, you've made a poor choice here. I don't know if you think you deserve this sort of treatment, but pull your head out of the sand before it's too late. No one likes him, not me, not your friends, not your kids. He's cheating in front of your face. He hasn't even been over to see your new place, you need to be slotted in to his schedule. You then run over to his place. Can't you see he's keeping you neatly packed away like a Russian stacking doll? He only takes bits of you out when he wants to play and when it's convenient to him. Keeping you neatly compartmentalised in a box only works for a short time," she said.

"I curiously took a peek at his profile once and he's got selfies on nearly every post. I mean, the guy's seriously into himself. I wonder if he checks how many likes he gets and feeds off of those or maybe he likes to keep tabs on how many women follow him. Nguyen is looking for someone to be in a conditional relationship and someone who will never be able to have a say. He controlled you by using his charismatic charm to lie and manipulate you," she said.

I was shocked. Sharni was my friend who saw things in an impartial manner. I was surprised to hear her speak like this. I was looking for guidance, not a kick up my backside.

"I haven't finished yet. I like Dave, he's a fighter, and he fights for you. I've watched you in meetings, I've watched you fight at rallies and campaign for women's rights. I've watched how articulate you are. You're fearless and confident. Do you know people are actually intimidated by you? And some secretly wished they were you! Stop fighting for others for a moment and start putting the same effort into your relationship with Dave. If things work out then great, if they don't then walk away and tell yourself you gave it a real red-hot go. Remember when Tara at work had a crush on Dave and you were rattled. You didn't want someone jeopardising what you had. Dave had no intentions of going anywhere with Tara. Stop looking at Nguyen as someone he's not. Start identifying the real from the make-believe. Wake up, forgive yourself for looking at his messages, move the fuck along. You haven't been charged with murder. Stop punishing yourself over something so menial," she said.

"Can't you see you're replaceable to him, but irreplaceable to Dave? Dave can't live without you and Nguyen can't live without a woman in his life, regardless of who that may be. That's not very special is it? Get rid of him!"

Our Thai noodles and spring rolls arrived. I dipped one in soy sauce and ate it. I began to feel unwell. My stomach had become so sensitive these days I could barely eat anything anymore.

Sharni sensed I wasn't feeling well.

"Em, I'm sorry for being so blunt. I don't usually swear, but you seem to be worshiping this guy. Hey, do you know the story of the Roman Emperor Frederick II?" Sharni asked.

"Yes. Why?" I asked.

"Nguyen is beginning to remind me of him. He had lots of lovers and he was married three times, but he was a nut-job," she said.

"Yeah, I know it well. I was haunted by the story when my father told me about red headed Fred as a child. I remembered crying after hearing it. I found it unimaginable someone could be so cruel. I couldn't get my head around it as a kid myself. Taking babies away from their mothers and putting them in a room, forcing the wet nurses to only feed them and not speak or hold them. Cutting out the emotional attachment. He thought they would grow up speaking a natural language without ever being spoken to. But the language they needed the most was love. That was the main ingredient missing from their short little lives. They all died," I said.

"Em, can't you see what Nguyen is doing to you? He's denying you the same attention and love those babies needed to survive. You're an adult and he's depriving you of love.

Those babies died because they didn't have the emotional attachment. He's slowly killing you too, with his games. The way he's treating you is entirely inappropriate. He's slowly starving you of attention. He comes to you only when it's convenient to him. You're left wondering where you stand. You don't know from one week to the next. Get out Em, before it's too late."

I was sitting twirling my Thai noodles on my fork, slowly eating one strand at a time, digesting Sharni's advice.

"I can't eat this food anymore. Since they've changed the menu here, I think they've started using MSG. Nuts and MSG are no good for me," I said, pushing my plate away.

CHAPTER 23

GETTING LEIS

I was raised to own up and take responsibility for my misdoings in life. I was taught to own my errors, come clean, apologise and move on. As a child I was made to go to confession even though I didn't want to go. I would become anxious because I never quite understood how to show true sorrow when it wasn't there. I felt bad making stuff up. I'd spend weeks ahead of time preplanning for my Sacrament of Penance to help curb my anxiety.

I recalled once when I was in the confessional box Father Vincent asked what I was there seeking forgiveness for. I didn't really have anything to say, I was ten years old. My father made me go to confession so I made up a story. I told him it was because I had found where my mother had hidden the chocolate covered peanuts she kept for when visitors came and I ate them all. I convincingly told him I lacked the strength to resist and overcome temptation. They were far too mouth-watering for me not to. I didn't really eat them. I had found them, but I knew it was the wrong thing to do. As tempted as I was to rip open the packet, I shut the cupboard door instead, and tried really hard to forget I saw them. I loved my mother and I didn't want to upset her. I knew she bought treats for special occasions only. I knew I would eventually be able to eat them when the time was right.

I felt so bad that I had lied to Father Vincent that I went straight back to church the very next week and confessed my sins. I remembered that day well. It was pouring with rain and I had arrived soaking wet. I thought it was God punishing me for lying. I was so upset I began to cry as I confessed my sins. I was truly sorrowful.

When Father Vincent came over for lunch that weekend, he handed me a packet of chocolate covered peanuts. He said I had a kind heart and I didn't have to make up stories for the sake of seeking forgiveness because God forgives all, and forgiveness starts within. He said that I deserved treats now and then too and the fact that I owned up took real courage and strength. He also said at ten years of age there really wasn't a need to go and confess anything and he'd speak to my father about it. He said I didn't have to go to confession anymore until I was much older. He said I might have real reasons then.

I had decided to tell Dave I was seeing someone. I didn't want to lead him on. I had too much respect for him. Some may have found this awkward to do, but Dave was different. It never felt difficult speaking to him. He never stopped fighting for our relationship and at times it became frustrating. Maybe secretly I thought this type of conversation might be what was needed to cut all ties with him once and for all. I was hoping this might be all he needed to hear to finally turn his back on me.

He wasn't giving me a chance to move on. He hadn't shown any anger or resentment towards me, only love. And this is what I was struggling with. He wasn't making it easy for me to turn my back on us. He hadn't given me a real reason to completely shut him out. Our friends and family were all secretly hoping we would make things work again, but I hadn't forgotten the real reason why I had left in the first place.

They say time heals all wounds, but I wasn't moving on. Dave was, within himself. He was thriving. He saw a future, a bigger better one which included me. He was improving and changing for us. He had stopped drinking and owned his bad behaviour. I was still struggling and consumed with my relationship with Nguyen. Although I thought I loved him, he wasn't transparent or open as he proclaimed to be. He was dramatic and tortuous, full of twists and turns, mainly within himself. I wasn't one to give up, and I was still fighting, but I think I may have been fighting for the wrong relationship. My time and energy were being sucked up by Nguyen.

"Dave, can we please catch up for dinner when it suits you?" I asked when I rang.

"Of course we can, how about tonight, at our favourite Italian restaurant?" he suggested.

"Sure," I said.

Our favourite Italian restaurant was really at home in our kitchen. Dave bought me a fridge magnet once that said exactly those words. He said I was the best cook there ever was, a real ten-out-of-ten. He gave me a nine once, he said it was to leave room for improvement, and I completely lost it at him. He stuck to tens from that day on.

Our favourite Italian restaurant was a tiny little café run by an elderly couple who made everything they served themselves in-house. This was the same restaurant where Dave and I had our first date. They were a cute elderly couple who were in their early 70's. The café looked the same as the day it opened, thirty years ago.

The tablecloths were red and white checks. Each table had a candle dripped in heavy wax stuck in empty recycled bottles of vino. There weren't many tables, most likely unable to deal with demand that came with large numbers of customers. The café was quaint and quiet. Everything as delicious as the first time I ate there. Nothing had changed, it was like time had stood still.

The waiter seated us and took our orders, the same food each time. Pizza Calabrese to share as an entrée and Dave's favourite tortellini alla panna as a main and I'd have the spaghetti marinara.

He put down a bottle of Italian sparkling water on our table and left.

"Dave have you ever thought about dating anyone?" I asked.

"Why would I date anyone? I don't want to go out on dates. Why would I go out looking for love when I know where love is?"

I looked at Dave, I felt a little twinge inside of me.

"You should date Tara sometime." I briefly thought about her and was surprised her name came to me so quickly.

"She'd jump at the chance," I suggested.

"That nut, no thanks. I'm happy working on myself for the time being. Where's this conversation leading?" he asked.

"Dave there's something I have to tell you. I've been seeing someone," I said.

"I know," he said.

"How?" I asked surprised.

"Em, I've known you since you were 18. You've been on this constant search mission in life. You've read that many self-help books, you'd just about be qualified to write your own. I'd be surprised if you weren't seeing anyone. I don't know what it is that you're looking for. Help me understand, tell me," he said.

"I don't know, I've always thought I wasn't good enough as a person, labelled as a mother and a wife. I haven't felt loved or appreciated by you for so long. I guess I feel that I deserve to be loved by someone. I know Nguyen loves me," I said.

"Bullshit! If you were in a loving relationship you wouldn't look the way you do, exhausted. Has he given you any direction as to where your relationship is headed? What's he waiting for?" Dave asked.

"Nguyen seems to think I'm in limbo, he's waiting for me to sort myself out," I said.

Dave began to laugh, he laughed so hard the sparkling water in our glasses jiggled.

"Emmie, I love you so much. I'm giving you the space you've asked for. We both know I have a drinking problem and I am getting help. I have an illness and I've acknowledged this. I'm moving forward in my life. I'm making conscious choices to help myself. I hope you start to move forward with yours too. Don't look for love through this guy, love yourself enough to want to make changes for you. You're not in limbo. You left me and you've had to refinance your world to make ends meet. You left behind a castle, and all the material things that you've since discovered no longer serve a purpose in your life. That takes guts. You're not pretentious, you're authentic, but lost at the moment. I've mistakenly contributed to that. I'm sorry. You've already started to grow and enter into the next phase of your life. Don't let some loser manipulate you into thinking you're in limbo to make you feel bad about yourself. You're not a stupid woman who is simply going to run into the arms of another man for the sake of love. You're naïve to think he's not an opportunist and he's certainly honed in on you at your most vulnerable. You've settled for a tumultuous relationship filled with the unknown and unsure of what the future holds with this man. He's obviously not offered you any direction whatsoever. What's the real reason Emmie? Why aren't you living with him?" Dave asked.

I looked at Dave, I could see the sparkle in his eyes. They looked clear and genuine, not dark and murky like Nguyen.

Although we were discussing the new man in my life, Dave sat opposite me in hope that we will one day reunite. I could see it in his eyes, he was happy just to be having dinner with me. I missed our conversations that we once shared. I could share anything with Dave and he wouldn't judge me, he wouldn't label me. Instead he would guide and support me.

"It's my instincts, something doesn't feel right," I said.

"Does this feel right?" he asked.

"Yes," I replied.

"So, stop wasting your time with someone who's labelled you as incompetent, telling you that you have to sort yourself out, without being specific, it's not helpful. Saying you're in limbo is rubbish. He should look at himself before he casts the first stone. That's just a lousy excuse so he doesn't have to stop and look at himself in your so-called relationship. You have made drastic changes to your life, that's huge. What changes has he made? Oh, wait. Let me guess, he's all good."

Dave was right. I couldn't disagree with anything he had said. I was already doubtful where my relationship with Nguyen was heading. He was showing me one thing and telling me something entirely different. It felt like I was on his sidelines and not on our forefront of the relationship.

"Come to Hawaii with me, let's go for a week. I've been looking at flights and accommodation deals. I was going to go on my own, just to get away for a bit. Five days out of our everyday lives isn't much to ask for. Let's both have a break, no strings, no expectations, and sipping on virgin pina coladas. We'll go as two old friends. We can unwind and leave our stresses behind for a brief moment. How does that sound?" Dave asked.

The image of soft sand beneath my feet and being miles away from the drama that came with Nguyen sounded too good to be true. Hawaii held a special spot for Dave and I. We had once celebrated our tenth wedding anniversary there. Just the thought of getting on an airplane and missing in action for five days sounded so enticing. Nguyen wouldn't even realise if I went away.

"Right about now, it sounds too bloody good to turn down!" I said.

CHAPTER 24

STRIKE 3 OUT

Relationships can send anyone around the twist at the best of times. Not everything works according to our plan in life. We all have our moments where life tests us. It's our narrow mindedness that can be our undoing. I was raised to forgive and show compassion to others. I was raised to have strength and resilience and forgiveness. There's a flip side to forgiveness, you can politely forgive someone who's unintentionally done something to upset you. Or even forgive over a misunderstanding. There's also a different type, when someone cuts you off at the knees. Forgive yourself and move on, as that type takes greater strength.

Aggression on the other hand is a sign of weakness. This is where you'll tend to find the unbalanced. Don't keep offering those types of people an excuse to keep them hanging around. Don't discount bad behaviour. If they show signs of aggression, you will most likely find underneath that they'll only see what they want from their own perceptions. You're usually fighting a losing battle in these cases.

I'm not perfect and I had never proclaimed to be. I'm not afraid to admit that and I take responsibility for my actions.

I didn't hide behind the false likelihood of perfectionism. I didn't have a problem apologising.

My cousin Rosie was the dessert queen in our family. She took after her mother. She made the best Italian cakes and custards. When I would visit her in Melbourne, she would bake the week before leading up to my stay. I would end up increasing in a dress size, her treats simply too good to resist.

I took after my mother and I made the best soups. Whenever someone was unwell, I'd bring around a large pot of soup. Italians often use food to express their love for someone. They used food to help others heal.

Whenever I'd visit my parents the first thing they would ask me was if I was hungry, instead of a greeting.

Each time Nguyen was sick I'd make him soup. I took good care of him. Although I had broken up with Dave, I didn't need rescuing. I looked at Nguyen who needed the rescuing. He told me he had never been cared for by a woman before. Apparently his ex-wife was too busy for him and didn't give him much of her time. She was a lady of leisure and didn't have the same work ethics as he did. That had led him to become depressed. That's the reason why he started to gamble and drink. He told me all his ex-girl-friends were too needy or had serious psychological issues. He couldn't deal with them either. Perhaps I was the lucky one, the chosen one. I found it surprising a string of women had led Nguyen to the dark doors of depression. His ex-wife seemed to be a highly driven and intelligent woman.

He became sick quite often. I felt like I was making soup for him every couple of weeks. Because of his excessive drinking he couldn't sleep. He would be up all hours of the night. His immune system couldn't keep up. His drinking became a problem. There were times he would forget con-versations we'd had. He would contradict himself or become argumentative. He was moody, and lacked patience. He labelled most people as stupid or dramatic.

We were trialling living together. It was like living on a knife's edge. You really don't know someone until you observe them closely and you share their personal space.

It's like holding up a mirror to them and they see someone entirely different. They start to blame the people closest to them because they don't like what they see. From expressing simple opinions or feelings, Nguyen would blame me for being 'too sensitive', or accuse me of making things up, insisting 'it was all in my head'. At times I found him difficult to understand and stubborn. Other times he would tell me we were spiritually connected. I really questioned whether he meant the alcoholic version of spirit or the universal higher being.

He began to project his behaviour on to me. I'm usually a patient person, I grew up having nothing but time. Nguyen didn't like being on his own. This confused me because he was simultaneously pushing me away.

"Hi honey, I've got those books you wanted to read," I said.

"What books?" he asked.

I held up two books. "We had a discussion last night about these two books. I told you I would go to the library today to borrow them so you could read them."

"I'm not interested in reading those books. I never said anything of the sort," he snapped back.

"I don't remember telling you to go to the library to get them either. It's something you chose to do. You're imagining things again."

Nguyen's moods were like no other I had ever encountered. I clearly remembered the conversation we had about the books. I thought I was doing a nice thing. I thought he'd appreciate my gesture.

I wasn't the heavy drinker in our relationship. He said he didn't have a drinking problem. He would have a bottle or two of red to unwind each evening. There was nothing wrong with this according to him. According to Nguyen, people drank every night and I was abnormal because I chose not to.

I thought relationships were about helping one another through stressful situations. Nguyen was creating more stress to both our lives via his best friends known as Shiraz and Merlot.

"Have a drink with me Em, come sit with me," he said one night.

"Okay, just half a glass for me though," I replied.

I liked watching movies and unwinding together. Snuggling on the sofa felt nice, it felt normal. It was the one time we both sat in silence.

Before I had realised, Nguyen and I had watched a movie and drank our first bottle of wine in its entirety. I was starting to feel sleepy and must have dozed off. The warmth of the blanket and the wine put me nicely to sleep. I woke to find Nguyen shaking me by my shoulders, he was standing over the top of me.

"Emmie, time to go to bed," he said gently shaking me.

I saw that he had turned off the television. I saw three empty bottles of wine on the coffee table. I was trying to focus and get up off the sofa, but I had a dead leg. My leg had pins and needles. I couldn't get up properly. I put my hand up to Nguyen who was still shaking me.

"Honey wait, I'll get up in a moment," I said.

I felt like I was tangled up in the blanket and my leg wasn't moving from the sofa.

Within in an instant Nguyen stepped back. I saw the look of rage on his face. I was shocked and scared all at the same time.

"You struck me!" he said as he took a big leap back.

"WHAT? What are you on about?" I asked horrified.

I wasn't sure if I had heard correctly what he had actually accused me of doing. I was mortified at the thought, but perhaps I didn't hear correctly.

"YOU STRUCK ME!" he repeated, horrified.

"I put my hand out, as a natural response trying to get myself up off the sofa. I have pins and needles in my leg!" I explained.

"No you didn't. You don't know what you're saying. You've had too much to drink. You struck me!"

"I was trying to do a nice thing and help you off the sofa and you struck me. Next time I'll leave you there, you can sleep on the sofa!" he huffed.

I looked at Nguyen. Each time he repeated those three words I felt the hairs stand up on the back of my neck. I still had pins and needles in my leg, but the adrenaline pumping through my veins stood me upright instantly.

I felt like I was in a dark alley and some guy was holding a knife to my throat whilst robbing me. At that very moment I saw a truly unbalanced man, a very dangerous man. I had not struck him, nor would I resort to such physical violence. I realised at that very moment it was Nguyen telling the story, not me.

My instant reaction would have been to cry, but my instincts kicked in. I was getting used to his poor behaviour and his story making when he had too much to drink. I had to play his game or I would be in danger.

"Honey, it was an accident, my arm jerked, let's go to bed," I said.

I led him by his hand like a three-year-old who had fallen over in the playground.

When we got into bed, I moved as close to my edge as I possibly could without falling out. There was no cuddling or any holding, just silent tears streaming down my face. I controlled my sobbing so my body lay in complete stillness not to give away my crying. My pillow case was wet with heartache and despair. I lay in bed, too afraid to move and I asked myself why had I settled for crazy? Was this what I thought I deserved in life? I was strong and resilient. I was courageous and smart, yet I was choosing crazy over normal and safe.

I thought about how disappointed and sad my parents would be if they saw me now. I thought of how I helped others escape the same situations I now found myself in. I doubted myself, maybe I was crazy. Maybe Nguyen was right, 'It's all in my head'.

The next morning, I couldn't even look at Nguyen. I didn't know if I found him repulsive or myself. I hadn't slept all night and I was angry and tired. I was applying makeup to hide my dark circles around my eyes in the bathroom when he walked in.

"Hello beautiful, you didn't let me hold you last night. You wouldn't even let me touch you. You get so upset over nothing, it's always something with you. I can't control what's in your head Em. You're always making stuff up and shutting me out. But I love you, you're so beautiful," he said, as he kissed me on the cheek.

My instincts were telling me not to accept incongruent behaviour. Words and actions weren't matching up in my relationship with Nguyen.

I cringed when he used the word 'love'. This wasn't love. It was used as a poor excuse at an attempt to make amends, and for the manipulation to continue. For some bastard to control my life so I would become submissive and dependent on him. He was feeding me what he needed me to believe about him.

My instincts were my connection to God, a gift he gave me at birth. He provided me with the ability to see others for who they truly were. Not through sight, but through feelings. I had to remind myself not to be spiritually blind by Nguyen and rely on my instincts more and more.

I looked at his reflection standing behind me in the bathroom mirror. I smiled and thought to myself, I am beautiful, but you're seriously nuts.

CHAPTER 25

FAITH

Mother Mary so full of grace. I was raised using a reverent and spiritual approach to life. I felt blessed knowing I could choose to either pray to a man or a woman. I liked praying to Mary, I found my inner strength through her. I placed my complete trust in her supreme divine. I found praying to her comforting and grounding. She kept me safe. Faith moves mountains. You can't see it, but if you believe it you will feel it. Tolerance and trust will grow through faith.

Dave had decided to go on an overseas holiday with a friend. The breakup was taking its toll on him and he needed to get away. Soon after our return from Hawaii he thought I would move back in with him. I didn't. He never thought I'd move in with Nguyen. At the time, I thought I deserved better. Not knowing I had signed up for something entirely different, something so unbelievably incomprehensible.

My holiday with Dave was pleasant. He was respectful of our situation and we slept in different beds in the same room, like best friends do as children at a sleep over. I wished I was back in Hawaii with him.

I was envious that Dave had travelled overseas. My life wasn't getting any easier. I felt like a child picking up a hula-hoop for the first time and spinning excitedly for hours. Not wanting to stop, but then realising once the fun was over, the spinning was hurting my brain. I had made my bed and I had to lie in it.

Upon Dave's return, he gave me the most beautiful rosary beads I had ever seen. They were stored in a little gold tin with Mary on the lid. He had purchased these for me from the Vatican City. I missed Dave so much. It should have been me on holidays with him. It should have been like I had envisaged married life to be back when I was a teenager. Like all the books I had read, my life should have a happy ending too.

I treasured my gift from Dave. Each night I would lay in bed praying to Mary, asking her to restore peace in my life. The little gold tin kept under my pillow until I fell asleep.

Rosie was visiting from Melbourne and we had decided to meet up for a drink and dinner. We were going to a tapas bar in the city.

"Hi Rosie!" I yelled out with my hand up in the air, as I saw her walk in.

The bar was packed full of people who had just finished work in the busy business district part of the city.

"Hi," she said, as she made her way towards me and kissed me on the cheek.

"I've booked a table, let's get a drink at the bar before we sit down," I suggested, as we made our way towards it.

I stood behind two men. I was patiently waiting my turn.

One turned and looked at me. He turned to his mate and said, "Let this lovely lady through, we're blocking her way."

"Thank you," I said, as I brushed past them.

"So, do you come here every week?" one of the men behind me asked.

"Do you?" I asked impatiently.

"So, you come here once a fortnight then? You look like you're on the prowl," he continued.

"Excuse me? What a sexist thing to say! How do you know I'm not here with my husband or my lesbian lover or both?" I snapped, beginning to raise my voice.

I stopped and saw people around me had lowered their voices and were now staring at me. I couldn't believe the nerve of this guy.

Why was I 'out on the prowl' by simply ordering a drink at a bar? He moved away with his mate, sensing the anger seething from me. I was all too ready to continue on with our debate. I was ready to chew him up and spit him out.

"Idiot!" I said, loud enough for him to hear as he quickly walked away.

Rosie stood by me and we ordered our drinks. We sat down at our booth. I slumped myself down leaning against the window feeling defeated and hopeless.

"Emmie what's going on? I haven't seen you this down and short-fused since your mother said you had to have dried ice for your first dance at your wedding. You were worried about the asthmatic guests," Rosie said.

I smiled.

"Those were the days, hey. We thought we had real problems back then, look at my life now. Some loser made a sexist comment at the bar. How dare he. It frustrates me that in this day and age some men still have a fractured view of women. It feels overwhelming at times, like my life. I don't even know where to start with my own problems. I have so much going on at the moment," I said.

"I feel like I'm attracting situations that test me. I feel like I'm turning into someone that I'm not. I was never this bitter or cynical. I've lost who I once was."

"Start from the beginning, Em. Tell me what's been going on," she said.

I told Rosie everything about my situation with Nguyen. The inconsistencies that I was facing made me feel like I didn't know who I was anymore. My anger and confusion had begun to dominate my life as were my thoughts. Nguyen's expectations left me bewildered. I felt vulnerable and alone. I thought I was doing the right thing by taking good care of him, but we had different versions. I was beginning to feel exhausted. Love was exhausting.

"What the hell do you see in this man, seriously Emmie?" Rosie asked.

"I mean, you've always liked a good challenge but this guy is doing your head in and you're still staying. You can't fix him and you can't rescue him. He obviously has serious issues within himself."

"I agree, I'm confused at the moment, I love Nguyen," I said.

"No you don't, you think you love him because you've made up some story in your head that's not real. You've captured something that you're trying really hard to prove is real. This is your life Em. You have nothing to prove, it's okay to walk away. He's so deeply entrenched in his fictitious fabrication. He doesn't seem to understand real everyday issues that go with a real relationship. He's living a fantasy, but you're smart enough to see the real from the fake. Nguyen is not supporting you to better yourself. It seems to me he'd be happy if you just shut up and stay home. That's called a doormat Em. Time to cut the ties and rediscover yourself," she said.

"You think so Rosie?" I asked.

"I fucking know so! You've known this guy for two years, and already he's lied and cheated. No trust, no respect. He's made you look like the problem. If it's nurturing and direction you're looking for, you won't find it with this guy.

Have faith, find your inner strength, forgive yourself and move on!" she said.

"Start loving yourself, but I guarantee you can't if you continue to stay where you are. Nguyen will never let you. Geeze Em, can't you see there's so much better out there? Maybe you should adopt Renata's outlook on relationships."

I began to smile. "I wish I could. I really admire her. She would walk away without flinching," I said.

I sat there twirling my straw in my daiquiri. I began to think back to my childhood. I missed my cousins. I reminded Rosie of the time she had come over for a play date when were little. I was four years old and she was eight. I had tripped and hit my head so hard on the brick wall I bounced straight off. Rosie was so scared she screamed and my mother rushed outside. Instantly I had an egg-shaped ball come up on my forehead.

My mother ran back inside and came out with the butter. She slapped so much on my head it began to melt down my face from the heat of my skin. I was licking it off my face as it dripped into my mouth. Then she came back out with two ice cream cones, one for me and one for Rosie. She patted us on our backs and set us off to play again.

In hindsight I probably had a concussion, but my mother had done me a favour that day. She taught me not to stop and think about the pain my fall had caused me, but to move the fuck along. I now had the same feeling in my stomach I had that day I hit my head.

Rosie was right. I was letting myself down the most. Nguyen was bad for my health I had already developed a stomach condition because I was internalising my grief and pain. I had developed so many stomach problems it felt like a deep dark hole. I needed to heal and I needed to remove myself from a bad situation I had created, all in the name of love.

CHAPTER 26

FIEND

"**M**A ARE YOU happy with papà?" I asked my mother.

My guilt was built into my working week, not allowing me to spend much time with my aging parents. I would visit when I could, but I should have made more time and effort than I did. I found it hard prioritising aging parents, children, work and shitty relationships.

"Si, perché? (Why?)" she asked.

We were sitting at the kitchen table sipping espresso.

"Emanuela do you think happiness comes easily? Life is easy depending what you make of it. I do my thing and your father does his thing. I like to spend time in the kitchen, he spends his time in the back shed. That's my happiness, being left alone. But it wasn't always like that. What's wrong? Is everything okay? Are you eating right? You look very tired," she pestered.

"Let me heat up this pasta for you, you'll feel better after a plate of gnocchi."

She got up and walked to the pan sitting on the stove and began to heat up leftovers.

I was beginning to regret asking my mother for advice or insight into her life. I was looking for guidance and direction. I didn't want to eat. Food was not going to solve my problems. I had become resentful towards my mother because I couldn't have a simple discussion with her without it becoming about food. I understood this was how she expressed her love for me, but shovelling down Italian carbohydrates wasn't going to help me. Perhaps if my parents learnt the skill of talking and expressing feelings my emotional upbringing wouldn't have been so distorted. Maybe I would have made better choices in life regardless of the direction I had to follow. I wasn't offered strategies, instead I was injected with fear and guilt to do the right thing.

I felt deflated these days. The right thing had come at a price, my health and well-being.

"Everything's fine ma, just thought I'd ask. I've been busy at work that's all," I said, shutting down the conversation. I knew I had come to the wrong person for advice.

I began to eat the plate of gnocchi she set down in front of me to keep her happy.

"Emanuela, go home, work on your marriage. Men, they're all the same," she said.

"You should put the same effort into Dave that you do in your job. You take after your father. Perché (why) do you have to help others like you do? Help yourself prima (first)," she said.

"Your father would come home with all sorts of different people I had to spend my days cooking for. He used to make friends at the bus stop! Quell'idioto! (That idiot!). He'd feel sorry for people all the time, but he never felt sorry for me who had to cook for all of them!"

Maybe my mother was right, maybe men were all the same. Was I missing something? Or was her comment a cop out? I didn't believe men were all the same. I had met some arseholes in my lifetime, but I was also grateful for the men that had become lifelong friends.

I was engrossed in my thoughts, looking for a sign of guidance. I shouldn't take what my mother says literally. In fact, I should be more open to take my own advice on board and listen to my instincts.

My father walked into the kitchen. He had been working out in the garden. He took his straw hat off and placed it on the kitchen chair. He had his flannel shirt tucked into his pants held up with a leather belt. He was smartly dressed, even in his gardening clothing. My mother still ironed a centre pleat down his gardening trousers.

"How are you dad?" I asked.

"Emanuela, I don't like where this world we live in is heading, too much sadness, and too much change. I turn on to watch the news on television and there is despair everywhere. Lucky, we have you helping to fight for a better world," he said.

Although my father never admitted he was proud of me, it was through our conversations we had, that I knew he was.

"Go home Emanuela! Go cook for your children!" my mother said shutting down my father, giving him a filthy look.

I knew that was my cue to leave, she didn't like my father encouraging me to work on issues she deemed that were out of my control. She preferred to keep things simple and in-house.

My father's words had left me thinking. Life was changing. It seemed more unrealistic and morals were flying out the window even for our generation. Technology had become intrinsic in what we did.

Social media began as a tool to share life experiences and stay in contact with friends and family, but it took a turn for the worst. People's mindsets had been consumed with the negativity of the world, through individual opinions and news stories.

There were higher expectations and less time to cram everything in. Some days I would lock my phone in my desk draw or have phone free weekends. I couldn't keep up with the beeps, calls and notifications. I found them annoying, while some found it addictive.

I was beginning to find it difficult to distinguish genuine people. Social media became a platform to build self-esteem and everyone yearned for the acceptance and humour of others, but this was confusing to me. I took people at face value. I was beginning to think society was breeding a new generation of narcissists.

I enjoyed working in politics and fighting for social justice issues, but even that seemed boring some days. Where women once burned their bras for attention, I was now throwing my plastic chicken fillets out the window. I felt like each cause I tackled would be met with brick walls. Women were fighting for better opportunities in the workplace, but were burning out very quickly due to work-life balance issues. We were still perceived as the home-makers and care-takers even though some were working as CEOs. I was now spending more time taking care of my aging parents and my growing family on top of full-time work. Was this what my life had become? Was this my in-between before I died and went to heaven? *Fuck this,* I thought to myself.

I was paying rent and tackling the ever-growing issues of an alcoholic ex-husband and boyfriend. If I applied for work in a circus as a juggler, I'd probably win the job. But the juggling was an ongoing competition between my head, my heart and my stomach.

There were days I clearly saw Nguyen was bad for my health. I had removed myself from one relationship marred by alcohol and stepped directly into another one. Unbeknown to me, I was repeating the same lesson. I was the clown.

I had days where I was the one completely intoxicated. Not with alcohol, but smooth words from Nguyen and his seduction would turn me into a complete fool.

I wondered how my father wooed my mother back in their day. They didn't have telephones let alone the technology we had today. Maybe they made one another a priority?

Nguyen seduced me pretty quickly. He used technology.

I was vigilant when it came to using technology. I wasn't going to risk having my private parts for public viewing despite being privately sent. Nguyen was a risk taker.

He reminded me of a child, yet I still couldn't get enough of him. It was sickening because there was nothing normal about our relationship. I had my head in the clouds. I was too busy caught up in the competition for attention and failed to recognise I was fighting a losing battle. I was wasting precious time occupying myself with the fake and pretend.

He was addicted to social media, relying on it to spin his web to capture more prey and keep his options open. To him, the online world was real.

"You've got to do what's best for you, Emmie," he said one night, and then quickly buried his face to his phone, with his red wine in hand.

Nguyen was already doing what was best for him. I just couldn't see it yet.

People who were addicted to being online became selfish and used it as an unhealthy escape from reality. Fake had become faker. Were we breading a society that lacked empathy from over-exposer to violence and hatred? It showed the true nature of what that person was really like. Ultimately, this would give me a better understanding of the real Nguyen.

Fake and smile at work, but calculated and manipulative online.

What happened to normal relationships? What was normal anymore?

I once thought I struggled with my upbringing, but adulthood was far worse. I had too many things to contend with. Not only was I struggling within myself, I was struggling with the new digital world.

It didn't matter if someone was deemed as a good or bad individual, it was social media that was based on image and how many 'likes' you get. If you don't get enough, you'll struggle with self-esteem and if you got plenty, then you're ego driven. And Nguyen relied heavily on his daily dose of 'likes'. They made him feel good about himself.

Explaining real feelings to Nguyen made me feel like I was going insane.

He told me once he had high functioning depression. He had caught me researching the symptoms online one night and went completely mad accusing me of analysing him. I wasn't. I was simply trying to learn more about his disorder. Looking back, I should have been researching narcissism instead.

If I looked closer, I'd really see a scared little boy in Nguyen underneath his five foot-four exterior. I didn't want a little boy who played online games, I wanted a man. A real man.

CHAPTER 27

LUCKY GIRL

"Emmie, you're so lucky to have a man like Nguyen. Lawyers are so hard to come by! How lucky are you?"

"Emmie, you're so lucky to have a really good job. Good jobs like yours don't exist anymore. How lucky are you?"

"Emmie, you're so lucky Dave is working on himself, it shows real commitment. How lucky are you?"

"Emmie, you're so lucky to have such a beautiful family. There are so many dysfunctional ones out there. How lucky are you?"

Luck, what the fuck was luck? Was I lucky? What did luck have to do with my life? Wasn't it through my hard work and determination and the challenges I faced that enabled the outcome I had?

Each time I heard someone suggest that I was lucky, I would cringe. It was as bad as someone saying there's light at the end of the tunnel. You need a driving force to get you through that dark hole. For me, luck could best be described as a dark tunnel. I had to walk through it until I found the exit. For others, luck is not getting hit by a car when crossing a main road during peak hour traffic or winning the jackpot at the pokies. I would take luck as a personal insult when it came to others describing my life. It wasn't luck that had anything to do with it. It was fucking hard work. I was the driving force behind anything considered lucky in my life.

When it came to the men in my life, I got one out of three right. XJ, he was my shining star. Not Nguyen or Dave. They were still hard work. One was a lost cause and the other, a work in progress.

Nguyen and Dave were similar in the sense they both liked to drink a lot. Dave was working on his vices to save himself from ultimately drowning and salvaging anything left. Nguyen didn't care, to him he didn't have a problem.

Was I lucky to snag myself a lawyer? Nguyen was intellectually smart, but lacked the capability to socially interact with other people. If he had good social skills conversations would flow naturally, rather than from behind a screen.

My career was forged through hard work and determination to prove myself to Dave and to make a positive contribution not only on society, but to our joint bank account. I was lucky in the sense I had others who supported me. I was lucky to have family on standby when needed. But that's what families do, and in turn I'd do the same. I'd prefer to think of this as give and take, not sheer luck. I had decided my 'luck' had run out with Nguyen. It had finally reached its expiry date. My insecurities were going crazy, jumping around like a cat on a hot tin roof.

I had decided to meet Nguyen for coffee and tell him how I felt. My stomach condition was only worsening and my health was on a downhill slide.

"Nguyen, I've decided I can't do this anymore. I honestly think you need to take a good long hard look at yourself and work out what it is that you want out of life," I began.

"I don't think you're able to commit to one person. I think you've been on your own too long. I want to be in a monogamous relationship. I want compromise and trust. The fact that you're constantly surrounded by women indicates to me you would like to keep your options open. I wish you all the best," I said.

"Okay, fine. I wish you all the best too," he said.

I got up and walked out of the café. I was trying hard to hold back the tears. There was no explanation, no fight, nothing from him. I arrived at my car, got in and the flood gates opened. I burst into tears. I cried non-stop for three weeks.

Nguyen texted me three weeks later, out of the blue. I was at work and heard my phone ping. I opened the message and my heart skipped a beat and landed in my throat. He sent me a funny meme about crazy Italian women and their fiery tempers. It was funny and I laughed. He texted me again a few minutes later.

"I miss you."

"I lack motivation to even undertake the simplest daily tasks without you in my life. I never once said I didn't love you. I lack any motivation to go on without you Emmie," he texted.

I was so overjoyed I began to cry at my desk. I hid behind my screen so no one else around me could see or hear me. Was this what I was waiting for? An admission of love? How lucky was I to get another shot at Nguyen, I thought to myself. I possibly couldn't stuff up again, surely.

"I can't wait to see you again. I've missed you so much," I texted back.

That same night we made up for lost time. No words spoken, but the physical intimacy was simply euphoric. Nguyen liked to have a drink readily available. He built up a thirst whilst making love. I had my thirst quenched in other ways. I loved him.

"Emmie, I promise I will delete all those women from my account. I don't need any of them as long as I have you," he said holding me tight in his arms.

"Thank you, Nguyen, I love you so much," I said.

I lay there thinking how things were now going to be better and different for us. This was our fresh start. Just like the food I ate growing up. Fresh is best. I didn't care if he drank every night. What's the big deal anyway? So what, it's no one's business what he does. Dave drank for years. It was encouraged and supported by the Aussie culture. It was normal to have a few bevvies after a long hard day. I was happy Dave was working on himself. Nguyen didn't have a real problem, he drank to unwind.

I kept justifying the niggling feeling I had in the pit of my stomach. It was telling me his online female fan club was the least of my worries. I was dismissive of this because I loved him. I deserved him.

As the months passed, our relationship grew. His true colours showed. Like a pretty spotted mushroom growing wild, so toxic it could kill you. His words spoken did not match his actions.

Is this what luck represented to me? Was I missing something besides a part of my brain? Feeling dehumanised and disrespected. My self-esteem had hit an all-time low. I was living day by day not knowing where I stood in my relationship. The cruel silence became deafening between us. Was I being punished?

We went from a few days, to a few weeks, to now months without speaking. I was too busy beating myself up when I should have been defending myself against Nguyen. I had failed me, not failed us. He already did that.

My paranoia overcame me. Did he love me or didn't he? Was he a good person or a bad person? I began to feel lost, confused and totally out of control. I was raised to: do to others what you would have them do to you. Matthew 7:12.

So why was I struggling with Nguyen? The roller coaster ride was way out of control. My mental confusion was overpowering any rational thoughts.

I walked into work one day and saw a pamphlet someone had left on my desk. It was titled 'How to fix crumbling relationships'. I flicked through it. Certain words like trust, respect, equality, mutual decision making, jumped out at me and hit me in the face. I decided to stop what I was doing. I turned off my computer. I grabbed my bag and left.

I knew I had been replaced and discarded. My stomach told me so. I didn't call Sharni, I didn't call Rosie or Renata and I didn't call Dina. I walked until I found a park bench and I sat and watched. Not watching my surroundings or the children nearby kicking a football on the oval. I sat and watched my thoughts and what they were saying. The funny thing was my thoughts were being fed by my stomach. The feeling best described as a thick twine rope leading to my brain, completely bypassing my heart. My thoughts were telling me Nguyen already had someone else he was seeing and I would soon receive confirmation of this. I just had to keep quiet and observe. So, I did.

"Let it unfold," I heard them say.

Sharni called me a few weeks later.

"Emmie, I have to talk to you."

"What is it?" I asked. She sounded nervous.

"Emmie, I don't know how to tell you this and it's been eating away at me. I was having dinner last week at an Italian restaurant across town when I looked up and saw Nguyen walk in. He was holding some blonde woman by the hand. He sat down with her at the table, but before they took their seats, he kissed her. He didn't see me. It made me feel sick to the stomach. Emmie I'm so sorry. I had to tell you!" she said.

Complete silence. I heard every word. It was like a police officer knocking on my door in the middle of the night to tell me a loved one had passed away in a car accident. I felt like I had been hit in the face. Unable to process her words, I hung up.

CHAPTER 28

LOOK AT YOU

Nguyen SENT ME his final text message and broke it off the only way he knew how, behind a device. He took full responsibility in his text message, well worded to make him the victim and blaming me. Apparently, I was the cause of his depression and lack of motivation. He seemed to be motivated enough to move on quickly though, without having the courage to tell me.

I was adjusting to life alone and I began to love it. I finally had discovered the time to do all the things I wanted to. Simple things, like not working to a time frame when it came to family life. Simple things like catching up with friends, that no longer had to be factored into my family's schedule. I was living my dream, freedom. It felt like back in the day when I was a newlywed and had discovered freedom for the very first time. No restrictions, no explanations required. It tasted enticing.

I had also discovered the things I once thought were important to me were now not. I had so much 'stuff' I had disposed of when I moved out. The amount of money I spent on unnecessary items was a waste. I no longer needed material items in my life to progress into my next phase. I no longer needed labels to make me happy. I was already happy within.

I struggled at first with my breakup with Nguyen. I cried and I pined. It had left a bitter taste in my mouth. He had marinated me over time to seduce me into believing he was sweet and kind. But it was my friends that remained behind who helped me with my recovery, reminding me of the true facts. They were there, holding my hand and listening to the same story over and over, until my mind was ready to release it for good.

My growth through loss had enabled me to become a different person, an even better version of myself.

I wasn't a fan of living my life by clichés, but I did have one I kept tacked in my mind. Not to compromise me for anyone. It was my life and no one had the right to devalue it. My health and wellbeing came first. That was a hard pill to swallow. For me to put it into practice, I had to learn a very important word, 'no'. I had to learn to use this word without feeling guilty. It was like watching a toddler taking their first steps. Once I prompted myself to use it, there was no going back, it rolled off the tongue naturally. Women were renowned for putting themselves last on the list. I shifted myself up to number one.

I learnt pretty quickly after my relationship with Nguyen there are different groups in society. I learnt to identify those who did not hold my best interests and I quickly removed myself from their grasp. My new word enabled me to move on quickly and without fuss. I wasn't a megalomaniac like Nguyen. Perhaps I was a bitch, but I'd prefer justifiable bitch over experimental psycho.

I began to travel and even went interstate to visit an old friend in Sydney. Matteo and I had recently reconnected when he was visiting his home state. He was gorgeous. We had a great time together, he showed me the sites and spoilt me. But I wasn't connected to him like I once had been. I had grown into a different person and realised it was Dave who helped me become the person I was today. I loved him for that. I still loved him. Dave was changing and evolving into a better person. He had given up alcohol and was continuing with his treatment.

"I'm working towards becoming a better man," he'd say.

I was renting a little cottage not far from where I once lived with Dave. This would allow Chloe and XJ to drop in and visit anytime they wanted to. Sometimes they would stay for a week or so, other times they would stay with Dave. We didn't make a big deal of our separation because it was what we both needed. I had wasted far too much time thinking what was best for me was Nguyen. I was wrong.

Dimitri was coming over for a visit and coffee. For years, he would tease me about my choice of coffee beans and how he had some secret formula to sourcing only the best. He was bringing me over a bag. They had to be specially blended and dry roasted. We both shared a love of coffee.

"Ella, make sure you select the right grinding number on your machine for these beans, don't grind them too fine," he said.

"Dimitri, I think I know what to select on my own machine," I said sounding annoyed.

"Ella, don't stuff up my beans!" he said.

"I'll stuff up more than your beans if you don't shut up," I said.

He laughed. I looked at Dimitri sitting at my kitchen table. He looked like an elderly Greek man who should be sitting outside a café in Santorini overlooking the Mediterranean Sea, basking in the sun. Dimitri was my friend and there were times we had very little or no contact with one another for years. But he was always there for me at the drop of a hat. There was never any awkwardness or hostility between us when we'd eventually reconnect. He was a thorn in my side that I wore proudly.

I smiled at him.

I made our coffee and put some Italian pistachio biscuits out on a plate. He took one.

"Why are Italian biscuits so bloody hard?" he asked. "I could have chipped my tooth!"

I laughed.

"Stop whining, you didn't chip anything. You're supposed to dip them in your coffee first. They're biscotti, they're baked twice," I explained.

I sat down to join him. The chemistry we once shared was still there, but it was also different. Was this what it felt like to be a grown up? Did it take me until I was in my forties to discover this? I think I was once attracted to him because it was drummed into me by my father that Greek men were the forbidden fruit. My way of rebelling. Although Dimitri had aged, he still behaved like a child and I found it annoying. I wanted a man who stimulated my mind and challenged my thoughts.

"You're looking more like yourself these days Ella. When you first came to me about Nguyen you looked destroyed. I'm proud of you. You've moved on well," he said.

"I guess so," I said.

"You don't sound too convincing. Really Ella, what did you see in him?" he asked.

"I seem to be hearing that question a lot lately. I saw a giving, generous man," I said.

Dimitri pulled out his phone from his pocket.

"Don't Dimitri!" I said.

I knew he was going to find Nguyen on social media and I wasn't in the mood to face what I was about to be shown. I didn't want to see happy couple snaps. I hadn't seen a photo of him in months. I had no reason to. Dimitri was the one who told me never to think about him ever again and I followed his advice. Out of sight out of mind. I had put a zero value on Nguyen and on our past. He no longer existed to me.

"Ella, I've been busting to ask you, but seriously tell me? Look at his photo and tell me what you see, not what you want to see."

"Is this more about you than me? Are you offended or curious?" I asked.

He sat there with a stupid smile on his face.

I took the phone from his hand and I studied the photo. I thought I had moved on from self-punishment, but I looked. I handed him back his phone.

"Well, what did you see?" he asked.

"A creep," I said with a genuine smile.

'What the fuck was I thinking?' I thought to myself. Nguyen genuinely looked like a creep, someone I wouldn't have touched with a ten foot pole in my previous life.

"Ew, I can't believe I had sex with him."

"Case closed!" he said.

"Ella, you're a very giving person, and I'm going to tell you how guys like him take advantage of women like you. Nguyen was a taking person. He liked the thrill of the chase, he saw you as a conquest. I'm sure his feelings ran deep for you at some point, but were short lived because it wasn't love. It was infatuation and lust. Love takes time to build on. You don't keep jumping from one to the next. He used you to gain some sort of benefit for himself. He saw a strong resilient woman. By being with you he was hoping to adopt those qualities. It's easier for him to try and break down someone like you to make himself feel strong and resilient. But he's a weak man, that was never going to happen. I bet he couldn't even keep it up in bed. I bet his issues ran right down from his head to his groin. Once you get past the exciting period of a relationship, what are you left with? You get comfortable and complacent. He can't handle comfortable, guys like him have insatiable egos. He got bored so he moved on to his next victim. You were fighting a losing battle. He can't live with normal aspects to a relationship because he's not normal."

Dimitri took a sip of his coffee. He paused with a silly grin on his face.

"If we were together, I know you'd treat me like a king!"

"Wishful thinking, Greek boy," I said.

"Ella, the guy is a creature of habit and he will repeat the same lessons over and over. I'm not telling you this to make you feel better, I'm telling you the truth. You were collateral damage. You were the fallout from him not being able to deal with real maturity. You were a transaction. And when he discovered you had a voice, he deemed you as difficult. He can't handle you having an opinion or answering back. So, the transaction becomes null and void. I find you challenging, I love your temperament, it keeps me on my toes, but some guys can't handle that. It brings up more about themselves than the relationship itself."

"I understand Dimitri. I grew up with an authentic view on love, it was real and edgy, you know in true ethnic style. Loud and getting your point across," I said.

"Em, love can be the best feeling in the world or the worst. It's about taking a risk and putting your best foot forward, sharing your vulnerabilities with another. You've been hurt by someone who played you by your vulnerabilities. He was waiting for you to stuff up so he could condemn you for it. That's no way to live your life. I know you probably felt humiliated once you found out it was over, but it was actually disrespect you should have felt."

I thought for a moment. Dimitri was right. It was disrespectful what had happened to me and how I had been treated. I didn't deserve it.

"Em, they say love is in the eyes of the beholder, you were just looking in the wrong places. I'm glad you've finally woken up from this nightmare. There might be days you will still question what happened, but keep reminding yourself of the pain you felt when you found out he was getting married. Betrayal hurts," Dimitri said.

"Betrayal sucked the life out of me Dimitri. It was the kind of pain I wouldn't wish upon my worst enemy."

"Dave is still there for you as am I. Nguyen wouldn't be able to handle all that class and fiery Italian attitude that comes with you anyway. That would take real athletic qualities and teamwork. He's not a team player, he's just a player," Dimitri said with a smirk.

CHAPTER 29

YO-YO DIETING

I WAS DESTINED to be a dieter. I grew up hearing, "Does this make me look fat?"

I went to an all-girls high school and that seemed to be the six-word loaded question. When I got married I would ask Dave the same thing. In the beginning he politely kept to his standard answer, "No." I stopped asking when he stopped looking above the newspaper to reply. With each diet I undertook and with each weight loss journey, I seemed to fall off the wagon and then get back on. Sometimes I would blame it on life stress, but mostly I would pick myself up and move on.

My 'in-between' began when my relationship with Nguyen ended and before my relationship with Dave resumed.

I was out with work colleagues one evening at a wine tasting event in the city. I wasn't really in the mood to socialise, preferring to spend time alone at home. I made the effort because I was told by Nguyen once too often 'I had to go find myself', and according to him you can't do that by sitting at home.

I met my friends at the venue. It was an old warehouse that had been converted and refurbished to look like an emulsion of modern, urban and industrial decor. The exposed brickwork reminding me of the rise of trendy pubs in the city. The room had strings of light globes from one end of the ceiling to the other offering a soft, welcoming glow. The tables were lined up so people could taste various wines. There were wine glasses neatly positioned in rows that sat perfectly on crisp white tablecloths. As people walked in, they were handed a glass and a score card with a lead pencil.

There were a number of people attending, mainly men. I made my way around the room chatting with the winemakers and marking my wine card. I felt like I was at a game of bingo tightly holding on to my lead pencil. I was numbering my favourite tastings when I looked up to see someone starting at me.

I had noticed a particularly good-looking man when I had arrived. He seemed to be following me around the room. He kept blowing his nose and that's what initially drew my attention to him. I couldn't stand nose sniffing. It irritated me as much as someone chewing loudly at the dinner table. There were certain annoyances in life that caused me to screech within my own mind. I was bored and trying hard to ignore him while my friends were off doing a masterclass. I convincingly encouraged them to go.

I had someone follow my every move that seemed too timid to approach me, so I decided to mix it up a little and have some fun on my own.

I waited for my shadow to approach me and when he was close enough, I abruptly turned into him purposely dropping my score card and lead pencil.

"I'm so sorry, I didn't see you standing there," I said.

"No, it was my fault, you have nothing to apologise for," he said sniffing his nose.

I extended my hand to shake his.

"Hi, I'm Emmie."

"Hi, I'm Ted," he said.

Ted and I began to talk. He told me he was a used car salesman. He was recently separated from his wife. He had caught her cheating with a friend of the family. He had one adult child and liked to drink red wine. He played badminton in his spare time and liked to travel. I was trying hard to be polite, engaging in conversation trying not to ask inane questions. I would rather have been sitting at home with a bag of corn chips and homemade avocado dip, but I wanted to make an effort. I wanted to prove to myself I was still desirable to a man. In hindsight, I was better off finding a hobby to fill my empty void.

It was hard trying to fake it with Ted, because I found him extremely boring. Being on my best behaviour on a Friday night after a long week when everyone around me was let-loose made me wish I had never agreed to go out in the first place. He had an annoying habit of sniffing his nose and it was constantly running like a tap. '*Blow that fucking nose!*' my mind was screaming.

My mind briefly thought back to how I once spent Friday nights with Nguyen. He was now sharing these with someone else. With each question Ted asked me about my personal life, my mind wandered to thoughts of Nguyen. I was wondering if he was out having dinner with his new fiancée or if they were snuggled up on the sofa like we once had, watching a movie and sipping wine. Sharing the same bed, we once had. I had been replaced. I was disposable like the box of tissues Ted would undoubtedly use daily.

I was sipping wine out of an excessively large glass talking to a stranger about his Shar Pei dog. I was politely smiling and nodding my head while my mind was convincing me some owners actually did look like their dogs. I could see this in Ted. He had a blueish tongue probably from all the red wines he had tried. He had a stocky build. He was short, with light coloured hair, and a deep-set wrinkled forehead. He had short pointy ears that stuck out from the side of his head. He wore jeans with a white and navy spotted shirt with a tan coloured blazer. Ted and I swapped numbers at the end of the night. I thought he seemed okay, and I guess I welcomed the distraction. I couldn't get Nguyen or Dave out of my head.

Ted called me a few days later and invited me out for a drink. We met one night after work at a little wine bar in the city. He was smartly dressed. I liked a man who took pride in his appearance. He actually looked quite tempting. We were sitting in a booth and he sat next to me. He was softly spoken and very polite. After a few drinks he seemed to cosy up even more and his confidence grew, along with my temptation. He began with his hand on my arm, and then it landed on my leg. His arm quickly made its way around my waist. I didn't mind. Although I wasn't drawn to Ted to a great extent, he seemed harmless enough. I felt rather sorry for him because at his age getting back into the dating scene must have been daunting. Maybe I thought I was doing Ted a favour, showing him empathy.

In no time at all Ted began to kiss me. He leant over and caught me unexpectedly. It was terrible. I was horrified that a man in his early fifties was so inexperienced. His tongue felt like it was fishing for a gold tooth filling that had fallen in my mouth, nowhere to be found. It spun around like the little plastic fan I kept plugged into my computer at work to keep me cool during hot flushes. I couldn't get him off of me quick enough. The only thing Ted offered me was a distraction from my life and a few complimentary wines. Just like Nguyen's online friends offered him, a pastime. My relationship with Ted was never going to work long-term. I was desperately hoping Ted was more experienced in other areas, unlike his kissing.

"Emmie, let's go back to my place, we can continue this at Hotel Ted's," he said.

"Okay, let's go," I said giving him the benefit of the doubt.

Ted lived in a luxury townhouse. It was spotlessly clean and beautifully decorated. It was minimalistic with the latest urban furnishings. His lounge room had a beautiful black and white print hanging from the wall of the Roman colosseum. His bedroom upstairs had scented candles on the bedside tables. He had a pretty velvet embossed bed head.

He didn't strike me as someone who had a lot of women over, rather someone who preferred to go to bed with a good book and a hot toddy. I saw hardcover novels stacked by his bed and a framed photo of his dog. I scanned a few of the books, but there wasn't anything I would read. He was into murder mysteries and historical fiction.

Ted quickly undressed. I was surprised at the speed he removed his clothes. He lay on top of his bed in his starkness. I was taken aback. My hand placed on my chest in shock. He didn't seem unfit fully clothed, however undressed he had folds of skin. He looked like his Shar Pei dog in the photo by his bed. I quickly walked over to the light switch. I turned off the lights hoping it might take my imagination to a better place in the dark. Something my cousin Renata once taught me.

We began with foreplay and it was as terrible as his kissing. I had to give him step by step instructions. I took his hand and led it on a guided tour. Between his sharp fingernails and lack of confidence, I was becoming frustrated and bored.

Sex with Ted was abysmal. He had a constant runny nose. He explained he had a medical condition called rhinorrhoea. It sounded like he was crying whilst trying his hardest to please me. I felt like I was consoling a lost child. He stretched his arm over me more times to the tissue box by his bed than he did trying to please me in the southern regions of my body.

"Don't feel bad Ted, it's okay, these things happen," I said trying to be polite.

'Actually, they don't!' my mind retaliated.

He told me he was into role playing. I felt like the only role playing I wanted to be a part of was if I were able to step into a time machine and completely vanish into thin air. I could no longer tolerate the biology class I was teaching or the nose sniffing. My frustrations got the better of me. I got up and quickly made up an excuse to depart. I promptly dressed and made my way downstairs to the front door. Ted followed me hoping to convince me to stay, but I had learnt my lesson and I knew this distraction had run its course, just like his nose.

"Sorry Ted, I have to leave. I've had so many missed calls from my kids on my phone," I said as I was putting on my shoes.

"My son hasn't been well so I better get home and check on him," I said grabbing my bag.

"I'm sure they will be fine, please stay Emmie," he pleaded.

I couldn't even look at Ted, I turned my head. He hadn't put any clothes on. I couldn't stand staring at his folds. I departed like a mad woman who had discovered antibacterial shower wipes for the first time and had to get home to try them out. Promising to magically remove all residues and mould from the glass shower screens, I knew I had to remove Ted's naked image from my mind. My attempted sexual liberation failed miserably and so did my botched attempt to forget my past. I should have tried hypnotherapy instead.

Ted tried calling me for a few weeks after that. I had to give him credit where due, he didn't like texting, preferring to call instead. But that's where my praise stopped. Ted wasn't for me. Although he was polite and pleasant, he was boring and not my type. I wasn't into wasting his time or mine and I knew Ted wouldn't be too cut up with my departure from his life. He'd recover quickly. He suited selling cars. He had that look about him. Once you peeled back the layers, he lacked the confidence or experience to flatter a woman.

CHAPTER 30

VENI VIDI VICI

WHY DO PEOPLE place value on some things and not on others? Like a pair of designer shoes. Why do some become so attached to meaningless things? Is it because they're pretentious? My nonna sent over a gold necklace from Italy as a wedding present for me when I married Dave. It was the most striking piece of jewellery I owned and I kept it close to my heart. I was attached to her memory held in my special gift. Some find attachment through material items to fulfill a void of unhappiness. Spending money on big-ticketed items. My attachments didn't carry a monetary price tag, instead they came from my heart.

I was attached to Nguyen once. Not in a pretentious manner because of his money or status, but sincerely out of love. I had an emotional attachment, that led straight to his heart from mine. His job was his occupation and it didn't define him as a person. I was proud to stand by his side and be seen with him. A good woman makes an even better man.

Attachment can be devastating when that supreme cord has been cut for good. For some it would be like losing a pair of diamond earrings in the ocean. But for me it was different. Nguyen told me once when I broke it off with him earlier in our relationship that he was attached to me, and he loved me very much. He was confused about my decision, supposedly leaving him baffled and hurt.

He took great offence to my words. Worried about what others would think about him because he was seeing someone else at the time he had met me. He was worried how he would be perceived by Jess and others.

I guess he wasn't the only one who was affected by how our relationship would be perceived or judged.

Our coming together was totally out of the blue, even for me. I had met him through Jess when he was already dating another one of her friends. I wasn't expecting anything out of his simple friend request. I wasn't expecting to be love bombed or pursued. In hindsight it was a cunning disguise using the digital age to tempt me. I couldn't get my head around our relationship with an entirely different set of rules. I wasn't allowed to be the person I wanted to be.

I thought Nguyen had broken it off with his previous lover, but he hadn't. She was quietly sitting in the sidelines.

When I eventually found out the way he went about cutting off his previous lover, Nguyen had justified his actions by the love he felt towards me. He said it was because of his attachment to me that made him ditch his previous girlfriend. He said there was no right or wrong way how he went about it. She had to go. When I found out, it felt like I had led him to hurt others, and in essence his actions were my fault. I guess if it was somebody else's fault, he didn't have to take any responsibility when the relationship failed. He said I was too alluring to walk away from. He said the temptation was too great and he didn't like living with regrets. He had to give it a shot.

Our roller-coaster relationship at times had us breaking up and then making up only reinforcing Nguyen's fear of attachment. He would convincingly encourage me to give our relationship another go. I'd go back to him, choosing forgiveness over empty promises.

He told me he didn't feel good enough for me and thought he wouldn't be able to provide me with all the nice things

I was accustomed to having. Either way I couldn't convince him any differently. He had made up this incredible story in his head and ran with it. He said I had sophistication and class and through his eyes I was a lady of leisure. If he had looked deeper, he would have seen all the nice things I had was only stuff acquired over time and fundamentally meaningless to me. I was too busy helping others to worry about the latest pair of designer shoes that were in fashion at the time. I didn't place value on material items unless they represented some sort of sentimentality to me. I never spoke about the nice things I had. He seemed to spot these like an owl, a night-time predator. Nguyen failed to see the good in me.

The best gift Nguyen ever gave me was two books. He was so proud the night he gave them to me, neatly wrapped and nicely presented with a purple bow on top. He never thought I'd develop an attachment to my books. I loved them so much. I kept them proudly displayed on my bookshelf for all to see.

Nguyen was always buying books. Ironically his favourite books were on human psychology.

Nguyen's lack of self-worth ran deep. Or maybe it was all an illusion and he was a grand thespian. A lame excuse or maybe an expert in disguise at getting what he wanted.

He wrote me a letter once. I romanticised his words so much. When I read it, I cried. It pulled at my heart strings. Two years later I found it while cleaning out my filing cabinet at work. I reread it very differently. I read between the lines this time. What he actually wrote was entirely different to the story I had originally made up when he gave it to me.

Like every good author he enticed me early on in his narrative, leaving me wanting to continue the story to find out what happened next.

He was confused between his heart and his head, but certainly not between his legs. He had no qualms going for what he wanted without factoring feelings of others or his own personal integrity. His human dial was set to zero. He wanted me, regardless of who I was already attached to, it was a game.

It's amazing what attachment can do to one's mind. Like when you think you've lost something by misplacing it. It can drive you crazy looking for it. You either convince yourself you've thrown it out or someone has stolen it. Then one day when you least expect it, you find it by chance. It miraculously turns up. Just like the letter he had written me.

Nguyen's words were cheap and waffling. What we were doing felt wrong to him. But it didn't stop him from doing it or even beginning it.

"You deserve better," was some lame excuse he used, justifying his 'struggles' with his guilt.

He said in his letter he would miss everything about me, already detaching in fear of my rejecting of his words. He tried to sound genuine and authentic, but in retrospect he was most likely writing what he thought I wanted to hear.

When I found out Nguyen was getting married, I was sure he would buy her the exact same jewellery he had bought me. I'm sure he placed the same value on her gifts as he did with mine and his previous lovers. I only had to log on to be proven right.

She was gifted the exact same necklace we all had. He probably received the same reaction from her as he had from all of us. Kissing and swooning over him. She'd then share it with the world and the praises would flood in.

"What a beautiful necklace, how lucky are you!" the comments would read.

"What a great catch!" they'd go on to say.

"What an awesome guy!"

"You're so lucky! You deserve him and all the happiness he brings."

Yes, a lifetime with someone she'd never be able to trust with a long-standing history of failed relationships. He wanted a mother, not a lover.

He'd convince her they were spiritually connected and they were soul mates. He'd convince her she was the one, but really, she was one of many. He'd convince her she's his perfect match, and the rest just didn't live up to her. They would plan their wedding, having the big banquet he's always wanted full of MSG. She'd think they'd go on living happily ever after. When he decided he'd had enough, he'll divorce her and she will be left searching for answers, lost and alone.

He believed he was always right and anyone who didn't agree with him had no place in his life. The cycle of uncertainty kicked in and life was perceived as difficult. Love shouldn't be hard. Love should be given freely and from the heart.

Nguyen tried in his own way to make things work between us, when he had the time. I wasn't qualified or equipped to deal with nut-jobs and chose to walk away. I chose to stop wishing and hoping he'd want me back one day. I wasn't the one dancing in limbo. When he did send me his final text message, I couldn't be bothered fighting for him. He didn't break my heart. He left me with the greatest gift of all, my books.

CHAPTER 31

QUANTUM PHYSICS

"MA, WHY HAVE you got all your clothes laid out on your bed?" I asked my mother on my weekly visit.

Each time I visited, she would have an unfinished task. I would find a linen cupboard half emptied or old photos spread out on the dining table with the aim of putting them away.

My mother was always trying to find ways to occupy her time. Since the passing of my father, she had to embrace loneliness. If she accepted loneliness, then she would probably also have to accept depression and grief.

Her days became longer. My father had passed away five years ago from a massive heart attack. It ran in his family, his younger brother had also passed away from the same condition.

I believed we were all a blueprint from our parents and our upbringings.

I had watched my parents growing up and now as an adult, I realise both of them where on a search mission in life too.

One was busy filling her days with remembering the past, whilst the other was busy planning for the future, saving others he met along the way. I also realised both my parents were searching for love in their lives. My father was a handsome man who welcomed the attention from other women. My mother was beautiful, confident and quick-witted, her spirit lead men directly to her. Now that my father was gone, my mother relied even heavier on her memories.

"Emanuela, I don't know what the weather will be from one day to the next anymore," she said.

"One day its cold, the very next day it's hot. I don't know what to wear anymore. When I was a little girl we had four seasons. Our summer clothes were packed away and the winter clothes came out. The seasons have changed so much now. I don't know what is going on with this mondo (world) anymore. I don't like where this is headed, it's tilted sideways. Hot, cold, it's all the same," she said.

"Ma, it's called climate change," I said.

My mother wouldn't understand the concept of climate change. She rolled with change. We all did, otherwise we might as well move and live in a cave somewhere far away. Nothing stays the same forever.

"I'll help you sort out your clothes ma. I think we can come up with a better system than you've got happening now," I said.

"Va bene (okay)," she said.

My mother and I spent the afternoon sorting through her clothes. We sorted them in seasonal piles. I worried about her, she was aging and lived on her own. She was still fiercely independent and sharp as a tack. She didn't miss a beat but not having anyone to talk to must be daunting. She relied on telephone conversations, her television and the radio.

"How are you ma, how do you go living on your own?" I asked.

"Emanuela, I don't have a choice. When your father left me, I had to adapt quickly. It's not good for your mind to stay in the same place for too long. I try my best to move on. When I was a little girl growing up, I had to endure the Second World War. I will never forget those dark times. Even now when I am trying to fall asleep, I become so nervous lying in my bed thinking about those times. The

German army invaded and took over our village. They shot and killed my best friend Marianna. I get upset thinking about her even after all these years," she said.

I was shocked. My mother hardly spoke of her dark days growing up. I sat on the bed wanting to hear more. I realised I didn't know every facet there was to my mother. She would tell me stories as a child, mainly made up, but this sort was on an entirely different level. I knew very little about her friends she had during her childhood.

"Tell me about Marianna, ma," I said, indicating for her to sit next to me.

My mother pushed the rest of the clothes to one side and made herself comfortable next to me on her bed. She sat with her hands clasped in her lap.

"When the Germans came to our village, they stayed for years. They had set up points all around us. We couldn't leave unless we went through these check points. This was the only way in and out. We were only allowed to go to the orchards to pick fruit and then back again. They closed our schools and shops. We could not buy food. My mother relied on the apples I picked. Because I was the eldest child, it was my job. I carried the apples I picked in a basket on my head. I was thirteen years old and Marianna was my best friend. We both looked the same and were the same age. We had the same hair colour and eyes. We would go everywhere together because we were too afraid to walk alone in the village. The Germans wore big black boots up to their knees," she indicated with her hands.

"You could hear them coming with the big thumping sound their boots made," she said.

"One day I had to go to the village fountain to fill bottles of water and Marianna came with me. We saw lots of trucks filled with soldiers pass us. Marianna became scared and wanted to turn back. It was getting late and the sun was going down behind the hill. I had to get water for my mother so I decided to continue alone. We had no water left to drink at home. Marianna began to run home. I watched her leave. I was worried I should have gone with her. She should have waited. When I filled the second bottle of water, I heard a gunshot in the distance. It scared me so much I dropped the bottle and glass shattered everywhere. I took the bottle I had already filled and made my way home. I kept my eyes to the ground so as not to make eye contact with the German soldiers. I had to go back through the entry point. There were six of them standing in a row. They let me pass. All the way home I thought I should have died that day. If fear hadn't killed me, they eventually would. When I got closer to home, I heard Marianna's mother howling. She reminded me of a wolf howling at the moon. Her screams were long and hard," my mother said.

I was sitting on the edge of the bed. I was trying so hard not to cry. I didn't want to upset my mother. I could feel her anxiety and her intensity.

"Marianna was so scared of the Germans, she ran through the orchard home and not through the entrance we had to use. She was spotted running up the staircase to the front door of her home and she was shot. My best friend was shot and killed."

My heart sank and my tears welled up. I could no longer hold them in. I stood up and walked over to my mother's dressing table where she had a box of tissues. I picked up the box and offered it to her. She took one.

"Marianna's mother refused to see me after that. She said I reminded her too much of her daughter. I wanted to see her but I knew it would cause too much pain. I had to accept this. I wanted to see her mother because she was the closest person left that I had to my best friend. Her mother's screams still haunt me to this day," she said.

"I missed her so much, Emanuela. I shared all my secrets with her. I remember one day before the war began your nonno went to Rome looking for work. When he came back he had two diamante hair clips, one for me and one for Marianna. They were so pretty. We would pin back our hair and pretend we were movie stars," she said with a smile on her face.

Her face looked sunken and her eyes looked deep with hurt and pain. My poor mother was a child of war. Her mental and emotional scars left behind were deeply entrenched.

"Emanuela, the Germans blew up our railroad tracks. We didn't have trains pass through our village. People relied on the trains because they would bring flour and rice from the city. We had no food. We had to rely on the land to grow and produce our own, but we were limited with what we could have. The Germans were living with us too and they took most of what our parents grew. Your nonno had to be very careful not to be caught stealing his own food from his own land otherwise they would have shot him," she said.

"What did you eat ma?" I asked.

"We lived on stewed apples for months and when we were lucky enough to get bread, we would spread lard on it and pretend it was butter. There were some days we were starving and I had to go beg for bread from others in the village. We relied on others to help us. We all had to help one another from death and starvation."

I began to think how my life was easy in comparison to my mothers. I thought of all the times I imagined it to be hard, when in fact it wasn't. The only difficult part of my life was my inability to control my thoughts. This made me sad, I wasn't into time wasting and here I was, wasting time on meaningless crap. Searching for someone other than myself. I should have been proud of my upbringing and acknowledge my parents did the best they could raising me, with the knowledge they had. The resentment had to go, I was an adult now.

I got up and opened my mother's wardrobe. I pulled out the clothes hangers and began to arrange them.

"I should have died back then, Emauela, but it seems God had different plans. I don't know why I'm still alive, I don't know why I am living in my eighties," she said with sincerity.

"Ma, look at what you have achieved. You came to a foreign country, you made new friends and learnt to speak a different language. I don't know if I would be too happy if Chloe decided to move half way across the world to start over," I said.

She put a few clothes on hangers and handed them to me.

"The world today has gone mad. People forget the simple things in life. We don't need stuff to make us happy. People are always looking for something better, instead of appreciating what they already have. They throw things away and not fix things anymore. Everything has become easier to replace, including people. I could have left your father hundreds of times, but I didn't. I stayed because I valued him, I loved him. We invested in what we had. We took care of each other. People who replace others are crazy if they don't think the new person hasn't got problems too. I was happy dealing with the man whose problems I already understood. I had lots of men who wanted me, Emanuela," she said.

"Ma you should be proud. You and dad were a team right to the end. Tell me the story about the American solider," I said.

My mother's face lit up like a Christmas tree.

"Ah, the Americano," she beamed.

CHAPTER 32

VENUS

DAVE AND I had been separated for two years. We hadn't gotten around to making our separation official. Neither of us really wanted a divorce. We had different emotions tied to different situations and there were different degrees of hurt on multiple levels. No two people are the same and neither are their feelings.

I felt let down by Dave in our marriage and I was moving on from my emotional hurt from Nguyen. Dave was hurting because his drinking had turned his life upside down. His emotional pitfall was overcoming an addiction.

We weren't nasty to one another. I still loved him. His strength and resilience were the mirror image of mine. Mirror, mirror on the wall, he was the greatest one out of them all. Dave projected the exact same thing I already had within me. We were like a pair of old slippers, the ones you never throw out because you'll never find a pair quite like them ever again.

We were living in separate homes and occasionally catching up for dinners and outings. In my mind we were still great mates. In Dave's mind we were still married, till death do us part.

I looked at the time on my phone by my bed. It was 2 o'clock in the morning. I could hear loud consistent knocks at my front door. I dragged myself out of bed thinking Chloe had forgotten her house keys again. I made my way to the front door and the knocking continued.

"I'm coming, Chloe!" I shouted.

I unlatched the door half asleep and went to turn to walk back to bed. I heard a man's voice. My heart felt like it had stopped beating and my eyes widened. I felt instant fear. I stopped dead in my tracks and quickly turned to face the door.

"Mrs Smith, Emanuela," I heard

I pulled back the door and saw a police officer standing there. Oh my God, it's one of the kids. I was numb in an instant. I felt like vomiting. I was wide awake. Fear does that to you, rushing adrenaline through your veins.

"Emanuela Smith?" he asked.

"Yes," I replied.

"Emanuela, your husband, Dave Smith has been involved in a serious car accident. I've come to collect you to take you to the hospital," he said holding up his police badge.

I squinted to look at his name and his photo.

"We need to leave immediately. Would you like change out of your pyjamas? If so, can you please do it quickly," he said.

These sorts of things don't happen to me, I thought. I'm not equipped to deal with trauma. I'm someone on the other end who offers others compassion and assistance. I'm the person who cooks and prepares meals for others in times of need. I'm the one offering advice and sympathy to others. I couldn't possibly deal with this sort of emergency.

"Can you tell me what happened please?" I asked once we were driving to the hospital.

"Your husband was driving through an intersection and he collided with a car. The car he hit was travelling in the opposite direction towards him. He had no way of stopping in time. The other driver was tested for substance abuse and tested positive for alcohol consumption. He was five times over the legal limit," he said.

"What? He wasn't at fault?" I asked.

"No," he replied.

"How's Dave? Where did this all happen?" I asked.

I was trying not to cry. I began to shake, my adrenaline had worn away. I was starting to feel cold. The police officer sensed this and turned on the heater.

"The doctors will be able to tell you more about Dave. I don't want you going into shock, so cover up with your coat. Take some slow deep breaths. The accident occurred not far from where your husband's office is. He had just left work around midnight. He was heading towards home," he said.

We arrived at the hospital and parked by the front door. He walked me in and spoke to a nurse at the front counter who pushed a button to allow the sliding doors to open. We walked into a different section. I was approached by a doctor. The police officer put his hand on my shoulder and I turned to look at him. He smiled and walked off.

The doctor led me into a room with a small sofa in it. She indicated for me to sit.

"Emanuela, Dave has been involved in a serious accident. He has serious head injuries. We've had to operate on him to stop some bleeding he had on the brain. We've had to put him in an induced coma. He's breathing with the help of a ventilator in intensive care. We don't know much more than this at the moment. He's not responsive right now, but with time we hope he will be," she said.

"What if he's not?" I asked desperately.

I had tears streaming down my face and I wasn't even aware I was crying. It felt like someone had turned on a tap. She stood up to hand me a box of tissues.

"If you are listed as his Power of Attorney, you will have to make some decisions around what is in your husband's best interests. I will need to speak to you about that later when we know more about his condition. Would you like me to call someone for you to come and support you?" she asked.

"No, thank you, I will call my daughter later. Can I see Dave please?" I asked.

"Sure, I'll take you in," she said.

We walked down a long hallway to the elevators. I began to smell illness and death all around me. The same distinct smell found in all hospitals.

We arrived to the brain injury unit. She opened the door and we walked in. I had to look hard to find Dave. He was surrounded by machines. The room was bright, but I struggled to focus on the man lying in the hospital bed. It didn't look like him. I approached him and took his hand that was by his side, uncovered. I stood by his bed and held it. He had tubes coming out of his nose and was covered in different coloured cables. He looked old and frail. His eyes closed and his skin pale. His head was bandaged. He looked like he had a three o'clock shadow, although he had most likely shaved the previous morning. I wanted to wash him and shave his face. I wanted to take care of him, but it was too late. He couldn't even speak to me. He probably didn't know I was even standing beside him.

There were nurses and doctors working around me, checking the machines around him and conversing, checking charts and scribing notes. With all of this happening around me, I felt completely alone. A nurse came to me with a chair and placed it by my side. I sat down. I hadn't realised, but my tears were still streaming. I began to feel the dampness on my top and it alerted my brain to force them to stop.

I had lost all sense of time. A new shift of nurses arrived. I didn't know if it was night or day. I began to question my faith. Why did God make Dave leave work the time that he had? Why did God make some fucking bastard drink so much and make him get behind the wheel of his car? He didn't even know he was driving on the wrong side of the road. What chance did Dave ever have? He would have been blinded by two massive bright lights.

A nurse handed me a plastic snap lock bag.

"Mrs Smith, this bag contains your husband's items that we found on him."

I took it from her. I saw his wallet in it, his mobile phone and his wedding ring. I opened it. I looked at his phone, it was still on. I looked through his messages. He had texted me just before he had left work, but it was saved as a draft. He mustn't have realised it didn't send.

"Emmie, I miss you so much. I've been working back late each night because I hate going home and not finding you there. I know I've fucked up in the past. I want you back. Take all the time you need. I'll be waiting for you. I've accepted our situation as it is."

My brain no longer had control over my tears. I felt like howling. I felt like screaming. My body filled with unthinkable emotions, I was ready to erupt like a volcano. My heart had torn in two. I stood up and I left the room.

I looked at the clock on the wall. It was 8 o'clock in the morning. I dialled Chloe's number.

"Ma, why so early, seriously I'm trying to sleep," she whinged.

I filled her in and asked her to come to the hospital with her brother. I asked her to call Sharni and get her to the hospital as well. I walked up to the nurses' station.

"I want to speak to someone now. That's my husband in the room," I said, sobbing.

I felt like my legs were giving way beneath me and I clutched the desk I was leaning on. My eyes began to see black spots in front of them. Like little planets orbiting the earth. I was blinking hard to make them disappear, but the harder I blinked the more tears I shed. The nurse came around and put her arm around me and led me to a sofa. I was sobbing so loud I felt like I couldn't breathe. I didn't understand what she was saying to me. I didn't want to be here anymore. I wanted to be at home with Dave Smith. Shock had engulfed me like a tsunami.

As a little girl I would make up stories, stories so convincing I began to believe them. I would then convince myself they were true. I had adopted the same trait in adulthood. Watch what you ask for.

I didn't like alcoholics. I perceived those types of people as weak. I didn't like to surround myself with weakness. The person who caused Dave's accident was a teenager who had a dysfunctional upbringing, causing him to turn to booze. The collision was so intense it split Dave's car in half. They had to cut him out. Dave's collider walked away with barely a scratch. Life is about the choices you make, regardless of how shitty you perceive your life to be at the time.

It was no use blaming God, or blaming my parents, or blaming myself. Because I had realised the person I had become was through the life I had chosen to live. God had bigger plans for me. I had to learn my lessons to help me become authentic. Sometimes he would introduce people into my life so I could see through them, the person I didn't want to be. Through the pain people caused me, it forced me to grow and figure out how to move on. The people who were meant to be in my life would always remain, no matter what.

The one thing that drove Dave and I apart had now brought us back together. Alcohol. Only this time, he wasn't the one who was smashed. He had been smashed up instead.

Dave was in hospital for six weeks. I refused to switch off his life support. I fell asleep one night by his bed holding his hand. He moved his hand in mine. Only ever so slightly, but enough to wake me and watch. He did it again fifteen minutes later.

Dave had to learn how to walk, talk and eat again. He was in rehabilitation for six months. His brain had to be rewired and nurtured again.

I moved back into the marital home. Life changed for us all in that car accident. I had to cut back at work and I relied heavily on family for support. My days were now consumed with driving Dave to his medical appointments and taking care of him.

I wasn't exhausted like I once had felt. It was strange, but we made a day of it. We had fun spending time together. We would stop off and have lunch or try out new coffee stops in between appointments.

Where once no one wanted to help me out, we had come back together as a team. Chloe and XJ would take it in turns to pick up the slack. From the mowing of lawns to emptying the bins, we all chipped in. There were never any questions around the love we all felt for one another. We had all become better individuals from the emotions and experience we endured.

It wasn't hard picking up where we had left off because we were both stronger people. The annoyances of the past were no longer that. We had grown so much that annoying things simply didn't matter. The 'stuff' we once had to have, we no longer required. We had all and more. We had each other.

We realised how much time we had wasted, looking for things that were already there. We were clouded by our ego and what we thought we deserved. We were pretty low on our own priority list, which only ever attracts the dregs at the bottom of the coffee machine. Once we had realised our value, things began to look brighter. We no longer had to fill voids through other means. We were confident enough to say no because we knew we deserved better. I once had my own limiting beliefs that the word, 'no' only belonged in the world of women. I had discovered this word was in fact universal.

Dave no longer drank. He chose to say "No" to alcohol.

I no longer gave myself entirely to helping others unless I wanted to. My void had been filled with self-discovery and love.

Now when I met people, I could distinguish who deserved my time and who didn't. There were no more debates with some loser in a pub or some egotistical maniac who was trying to change me. I would simply walk away, how I was raised to do, with class and sophistication. No matter how much wealth one has, you can't buy those qualities.

I understood why my mother had taught me to walk away in that manner. There was no point in putting up a fight with someone who didn't deserve to have me in their lives. Replacing someone will continue to happen with some people. Until they overcome their fears of attachment, they will not place value on anyone. Most people think they fear abandonment and loneliness, but really, they fear attachment. When you are truly emotionally attached to someone, then you realise how much they are really worth to you and the thought of losing them is unbearable.

I was happy to continue my journey with Dave. I helped him like he used to help me. Through his rehabilitation, he had become frail. His recovery would take time. He had sustained multiple broken bones, fought serious infections and had to have blood transfusions.

Love shouldn't be a need to be desperately wanted by another, impacting your sense of self and turning you into a dramatic nut job.

Love shouldn't include drama and toxic projection of our own demons.

Life leads us in various directions. I had met people in my past who I thought I loved and were on the same page. It felt the same for both of us at the time, but that wasn't the case. The other person changed and no longer wanted to be with me. I then realised it was a distorted kind of love, the sort that was too painful to process. Acceptance and moving forward is the only key to unlocking peace within.

Relationships shouldn't induce cravings for attention, like the longing of a greasy hamburger after a night on the town.

Love should start within. Once I began to love myself enough I quickly realised when boundaries were being compromised.

I had discovered my love for Dave on an entirely different level.

I felt love on a different scale now. It involved taking the good with the bad. Working through issues and accepting one another. Familiarity began to feel good.

Not all the 'stuff' in the world could compensate for true and meaningful love. I no longer felt the need to seek anyone's approval for my relationship with Dave. I finally felt comfortable in my own skin and no longer felt the need to analyse our relationship. We had mutual trust, honesty, affection, and a sense of fullness like my homemade honey joys. Life began to taste sweet.

Although Dave was still healing, life became easier, not harder. It felt comfortable.

I actually liked Dave.

THE END

ACKNOWLEDGMENTS

Writing this book came very naturally to me. With each chapter I wrote, I found myself excited writing about the intended journey of each character. I was also supported and encouraged by my friends and family to continue my writing experience. I take great pleasure in mentioning and thanking those below. I am eternally grateful and sincerely appreciative to you all.

I would like to thank from the bottom of my heart, Shireen Khemlani, for always encouraging me to keep writing even on busy days.

My friend Donna Orchard, always there at a drop of a hat offering suggestions and solutions to my stories that have been most entertaining and creative. Thanks for her piece: About the author.

My editor Bianca Iovino, who put my book on a diet and still managed to keep all my work intact and forces me to think outside the square.

Special thanks to Ashley Khemlani for her graphic design.

My friend Sue Ryan, spontaneously suggesting better words to use in dialogue that make me sit up and listen. My personal thesaurus and coffee maker.

My friend Tish Champion, I wouldn't be writing at all if it weren't for her. Thank you for the many opportunities that have been given to me in the past.

My crazy multi-cultural family Peter Thomas, Alysia Thomas, Patrick Thomas, Joel Caon, Rosa Roocke, Yule Watts and Pamela Eastick-Watts, for your constant support and encouragement. I thank you from the bottom of my heart. You're always there for me. Special thanks to Patrick and Peter for helping me with my draft readings saving me hours of work.

On my Italian side cousin Rosa, for allowing me to share some of her stories in my book. I'm eternally grateful. Growing up wouldn't have been the same without her. My Dutch cousin Yule for unleashing the inner Chihuahua and giving me even more stories to write about. Pam, for her beautiful caring nature reminding me of inner peace and all the beautiful things that this big wide world has to offer. No challenge ever too hard.

This book would not have been possible if it weren't for the stories I was raised listening to. My cultural upbringing is something I am very proud of as well as the family values I was raised with. I intend to keep these stories alive through future publications.

Last but not least Dave Smith, thanks for being in my stories.

AUTHOR'S NOTE

Thank you so much for reading NUT FREE.

As an independent author NUT FREE is my second novel. The story of Emmie and Nguyen continues while expanding on the relationships formed in MSG FREE.

MSG FREE was published in 2019. My first novel explains more about Emmie's heritage and what made her who she is.

The main character Emmie explains further in NUT FREE how the relationships in her life have come about and evolved. She reflects back to when they all first met. She sees life in her own authentic way, preferring to see the same in others. She discovers this is not the case with some. She seems to keep attracting the same life lessons.

I feel like I have developed true and meaningful relationships with all the characters. I hope you can too. There is humour using cultural referencing and a true sense of family amongst some of the characters.

NUT FREE is set in Australia. Although I have mentioned Melbourne, Brisbane and Sydney, the setting is able to be visualised wherever the reader imagines.

I have chosen to introduce the character Emmie earlier in her life as she grows forth from a teenager into adulthood.

I wrote this book to reflect the strength and resilience within the main character. Therefore, hoping to resonate with the reader by giving examples of various life lessons. I also touch on multiculturalism in Australia and social media.

Please continue to follow me on Facebook: Eleonora Thomas Author and Instagram. I would like to share more of my experiences with you, new editions and future novels.

Thank you again for reading my book and meeting Emmie. I hope you love her as much as I do.
    Eleonora Thomas.

ABOUT THE AUTHOR

Eleonora Thomas lives and writes in Adelaide, South Australia. She likes to surround herself with good Italian food, wine and coffee.

She enjoys cooking up a feast for her family and friends who she cherishes. She enjoys living the hills lifestyle where she likes to hike and bushwalk.

Having known an array of mixed nuts in her own life, good or bad, she has learnt when to savour the flavour and when to spit it out.

A slice of wisdom she happily shares with any and all who need it.

She has two adult children who are her best friends and her greatest teachers in life. Although they drive her crazy at times, she still adores them.

Also by Author Eleonor Thomas

MSG FREE

An Italian's way of dealing with the artificial

INTRODUCTION

Happy New Year. They say that January is the carry-over month from December, the carrying over of rubbish in one's life and that the New Year doesn't start until February. Well, mine just kept going.

I'm Emanuela Smith, Emmie for short. I can't really say that I suit my name. There is nothing wrong with being a 'Smith', it is just something that I have struggled with in my adult life. I feel like I should be an 'Emanuela Donatello' or something more culturally exotic. I mean, one's heritage and culture are more socially accepted now than it was 30 years ago, and diversity is embraced.

I have big apple green eyes and long dark hair with pouty lips. When I think of my name, Emanuela Smith, I think of fish and chips by the beach. Instead, it should be golden strands of handmade spaghetti alle vongole, washed down with fine red wine. I was born to Italian parents, therefore carbohydrates are a part of my constitutional makeup, and I wouldn't have it any other way.

Life leads us all in various directions. It hands out lessons, like standing at the counter of an Italian patisserie shop. Should I have that extra chocolate chip encrusted ricotta cannoli or not? Knowing you cannot stop at one, you order it anyway. Was it the right decision? Will it make me fat? Where is my willpower? Am I being foolish? It's okay, it's no big deal. We are always trying to justify our actions.

The carryover of rubbish in one's life into the next year, and perhaps many more years to follow, will not end. If we do not learn our lessons, they will keep repeating. How do I know this? Well it just so happens I ordered an extra Greek lamb yiros once and the tzatziki sauce repeated on me for years. You see, my eyes can be a lot bigger than my stomach at times, and if we don't stop ourselves or recognise the signs it will keep on going…year…after year… after year.

Social media and its users are rapidly taking over the world, so much information readily available. It's become an addiction. We have meltdowns when our phones stop working. People turn psychotic when they cannot access their daily prescription of who is doing what. We hit spell check and pull out our phones to calculate simple mathematical equations. What happened to a basic knowledge of maths and English? We eat out and spend more time taking photos of our meal and posting them than actually enjoying the food itself.

Society places so much emphasis on who we should be, what is or isn't politically correct, how we should think, how we should dress and how many 'likes' we get.

Have we all gone mad? Have we lost our way? We seem to relive the past, hope for a better future and overlook the very moment.

I thought I had lost my way once. I was told I had to find myself. Spend time finding out who I really was in solitude. I am here to tell you all, you already know who you are. You do not have to spend time in isolation to discover this, unless you want to. Go climb Mount Everest if that's what takes your fancy. I know who the fuck I am. I'm not perfect nor do I pretend to be.

My journey or yours should be just that, independent of one another. Support and motivation from friends and family are what empowers and inspires me to continue throughout life, not judgemental antidotes, or what the latest self-help remedy is. It comes from within. We all know who we are, what make us tick, and *that's* authenticity, something I value.

Friends come and go. Family tree branches die, reproduce, and bear new fruit. The fountain of youth leads the way. We are all role models to someone in life, we may or may not realise this.

How we see ourselves and how the person you pass walking down the freezer section at the local supermarket sees you are completely different. Should it matter what people think of you? No, it should not. So why do we care so much?

There is so much emphasis on self-discovery, self-respect, self-worth, self, self, and self. Therefore, I am here to say to *myself*, start living. Forget about the bullshit in your past and start living the way you would like regardless of other people's expectations. You cannot change something that has not happened yet, and worrying about it will only reinforce something that does not exist.

Let's not become confused between our minds and our hearts. It's our thoughts that need observing. Expectations lead to disappointments and I am keeping mine real. I have punished *me* enough. Broken hearts heal.

CHAPTER 1

ROUND AND ROUND WE GO

"**H**APPY NEW YEAR!"

"Thanks Jess." Jess Thompson and I have been friends for many years. Jess runs her beauty salon at the local shopping centre and that's how we met. I have been a client of hers for years. Our friendship consists of coffee and cake and seeing the occasional blockbuster movie when time permits. We do not live out of each other's pockets, but we do call one another now and then to touch base on life. She and I both know we are there for one another no matter what. Jess has blonde hair, blue eyes and is always perfectly spray tanned, so much so, her nail polish on her toes look fluorescent.

"Did you hear the news? Nguyen is getting married! He's getting married! Some gold digger has finally snapped him up," Jess said, half laughing.

"I mean if it wasn't for his financial status you wouldn't look twice at him, right?"

And there we had it. Those three words. The three words that will lead me on the way to my journey of self-discovery.

He's getting married...

The heat began to rise from the pit of my stomach. I felt like I had eaten a second bowl of tortellini alla panna when I knew I shouldn't have, and I washed it down with a glass of corked red wine. The acid churning the warm cream.

Within seconds I threw up, my face poking into a lavender bush. The flowers brushing up against my skin. Still holding on to my phone, up it comes, the lavender scented acid. Funnily, I had not even eaten, yet I was throwing up a smorgasbord of food. I was not expecting to fertilize my lavender bush with vomit after I had only finished watering it.

"Emmie, Emmie are you okay, what's going on?" Jess asked.

I didn't know how to tell Jess I had been dating Nguyen for nearly two years. I had even moved in with him for a short time. I had hidden this from her and others. Nguyen kept me away from my friends, then dumping me via a text message in November. Now he was getting *married*. It was only two days into January. I was so ashamed. I was so hurt. My mind and my vulnerability allowed this man to control me in such a way. I had my reservations at first, but at the time I went with the flow. I made poor choices and now I was paying the price. Humiliation.

I had found out Nguyen was in a new relationship on Christmas day. Nguyen is the type of man who required his daily dose of one hundred and ten plus likes and word spread quickly. Needless to say, that was one Christmas I will never forget. No Christmas turkey for me that day, rather a large lump in my throat perfectly positioned to stop me from sobbing.

"Jess, I was with Nguyen. We were in a relationship until he dumped me in November." I said between sobs.

"What the hell are you saying?" I could hear the surprise in Jess's voice.

"Jess I love him." I said, trying to convince the both of us.

"You *think* you love him!" Jess snapped.

"Emmie, he broke Amanda's heart. Four years on, and she's still not over him. What made you think he wasn't going to break yours? His relationships have a very short life span," Jess said sternly.

Jess was right, I was more upset at the fact that Nguyen had used social media as an avenue to spin his little web to suck me in, and lacked the dignity and honesty to provide me with a face to face explanation at the end of our relationship. I guess he was simply a cowardly keyboard warrior after all.

Jess listened intently as I filled her in.

"I'm coming over to see you tomorrow, I think I need to fill you in on *our* Nguyen," Jess said sarcastically before we ended our phone conversation.

What is love without self-respect? Not much at all. Having no self-respect could be compared to a doormat. People use this to wipe their dirty feet on before they walk through the door.

I met Nguyen Xin through Jess. We were all mutual friends. Jess lived next door to him and his family when they were growing up, so she'd known him for quite some time. Jess would often innocently post pictures of us out and about on social media. Hence the friend request that leads to my journey down the path of Asian fusion and the spring rolls with sweet chilli sauce repeating on me. You can never just stop at one. It's one of those frozen foods you use when entertaining large crowds, it's a much cheaper option.

Nguyen had sent me a friend request two years prior. I still remember that day. I was lying in bed when I heard my phone ping. Sunday morning sleep in. I reached for my phone. I had to look twice, I wasn't too sure who the request was from. I was not a fan of social media, but hey, once I recognised who it was, I was okay with that. He was cute I guess, I was curious and now we were 'officially' friends. I hit accept faster than I could blink. I mean what harm was there in a simple friend request?

Checking out his profile was impressive. Single, gym junkie, sports fanatic, great social life, great sporting accolades, a human rights lawyer, lots and lots of friends. Who has over nine hundred friends? Where do you find so many friends? I felt modest with my one hundred friends. I could spend hours and hours researching this person via the information he voluntarily posted. He had lots of female friends.

It started with random likes from Nguyen, and then it went on to the random comments on posts. Days went by, the comments became more frequent, and then they found a new home. We began to chat via private messages. These became more common, and then they became daily. Was I excited? Of course, I was! Who wouldn't be? He was so seductively confident.

"Hello beautiful how's your day?" Nguyen messaged.

"Hi! Good thanks how about yours?" I replied.

"Yes good, doing things with the kids, work has been busy, can't stop thinking about your beautiful big green eyes, I just want to kiss you." He messaged.

"I think about you too." I replied.

"I miss you Emmie." He messaged.

Does he miss me? Does he want to kiss me? Wow, Nguyen misses me! I hardly knew him. He liked to move at a fast pace, but I thought I really liked him. I like risk takers. I liked the excitement and confidence Nguyen fed me. I like honesty, he missed me.

Nguyen was quite the charmer. In fact, he was so good he made me feel like I was the only woman in his world. Was I fooling myself? Could it be possible he was juggling more than one woman in pseudo-relationships? I am an educated woman, god damn it. I am forty-four years old. I am mid-career, working as an adviser to a female politician. If someone was going to play me, I would see the signs, right? Wrong! I was caught up in this pipedream called love. A fucking make believe fairy-tale where the narrator is an expert at not so happy endings. If it's too good to be true it most likely is!

We have been led to believe love makes the world go round. We all need it and we all want it. We seek it out as if it is something so unattainable. It is already there, within us. However, we need reminding. If I had reminded myself about self-respect, self-love, and most importantly, self-awareness with Nguyen, I may have recognised the signs earlier than I had, perhaps saving my chest cavity the scar it bears today.

He showered me with attention. Each message began with "Hello beautiful." I was beautiful! I will take that, thank you very much. No one had ever called me beautiful before. I began to feel like more than *just* a mum, or *just* a wife whom I was relentlessly giving to an ongoing difficult relationship.

There we have it lesson one in life, self-respect should not include the word 'just'. We are not *just* anything. We are all and more.

"Hello beautiful, I'd really like to see you, I'd really like to catch up for a drink, I can't stop thinking about you," texted Nguyen.

"Sure! I'd love to, why don't we meet at your local pub? We can have a few there." I replied.

"I can't wait to see you beautiful." He messaged.

"I can't either Nguyen, see you there." I replied.

Nguyen's eyes are so intense, dark, and mysterious. I could see the sadness they carried. I have always believed you can tell a lot about a person through their eyes. Why was this person sad? He had no reason to be, well not according to his social media profile.

He is a serious person, but I liked that. I liked the intensity. His sense of style is average, neat and tidy, nothing spectacular like I'd imagined a lawyer would dress. He has gorgeous shiny black hair. His quirky hairstyle reminded me of a cross between a sulphur crested cockatoo and the troll doll my cousin Renata used to have as a kid. He has a very trim athletic body and his legs a little on the thin side. He has the most beautiful hands I had ever seen on a man. So refined, they seemed like they belonged to a surgeon and not a lawyer, repairing and easily sewing up an artery with exact surgical precision. Each finger so perfectly defined he looked like he should be playing Mozart Piano Concerto No. 21 showcasing them.

I sat there in awe. Elbow on the table with my head tilted to the side. My chin was cupped in my hand listening to him, like a child listening to *Strega Nona* for the first time.

My hamster wheel went into overdrive, *he is so well educated*, I thought to myself. Listening to every word that came out of his mouth strung together like it was a golden thread. *I am so lucky to be here with him.* I thought to myself. *Why? Why am I the lucky one?* I then wondered, briefly observing my thoughts.

We had our regular hangouts, quiet little pubs, not too many people around. Intimate. Why should I care who sees us anyway? Was I that worried? I couldn't explain it. Was it guilt? Perhaps, but why? I deserved happiness in my life. I began to justify my newly found happiness. I was beautiful and that was all that really mattered.

"Nguyen, what happened between you and Amanda?" I asked.

I knew Nguyen had been dating one of Jess's friends before me.

"She's too needy and I can't handle needy women!" he said with such a cutting tone.

I sat up-right now, elbow down, the bar stool sticking to me making me feel six inches taller. I do not like men who label women. I am someone who fights for women's rights.

Protesting with banners in hand, waving them above my head for all to see. Where is my banner now?

"Needy?" I waited with bated breath. I wanted a reasonable explanation so I could put my imaginary banner down. He is too nice to be disrespectful to women, right? He has a mother and she is a woman. He is intelligent, he must understand women surely?

"She has no idea, she's a victim of her own circumstances, and she can't cook," he said with tone.

What did I just hear him say? My imaginary banner was flapping in the wind at this one comment, flapping so hard that it ripped in half!

"Oh really? What happened? Nguyen why are you so upset?" These were simple questions I was beginning to regret asking.

He went on to explain. He said her steaks were always overcooked, he preferred his rare, and she never put enough butter in her mash potatoes. Her kids were annoying, she didn't discipline them. She would overcompensate with giving her attention to them and not enough to him. Her children didn't have much contact with their biological father. Nguyen felt like he had to solve Amanda's problems and he couldn't be bothered anymore. His explanation was undertaken with such precision and persuasion that I readily accepted it. In a total of fifteen minutes, I was stargazing into his eyes. Explanation sufficient. It was like he fed me the most perfectly prepared crème brûlée. I ate it all up. He had been hard done by Amanda, it was all her fault.

I was on the road to love again. Nguyen made everything sound so much better. I thought he was so smart. I admire an intelligent man. I mean he had enough sense to pursue me, right?

"You, beautiful, are different. You are strong and resilient and you are not needy at all," Nguyen said convincingly.

Nguyen simply idolised me. He was so encouraging and caring. I was *all* and more.

Jess would mention Amanda and Nguyen in conversation when we had our coffee catch ups. Our discussions around relationships and others were a common topic amongst us. She would tell me how bad things were between them. How the pressures of the modern world influenced single mothers and how they were never going to work together as a couple due to his lack of understanding around this. She was busy raising a family on her own and he was busy pursuing his dreams. She would fit into his schedule when an opening became available.

So why should 1 care what happened in their past relationship? This was my future sitting right in front of me. I wanted to support Nguyen now and Amanda had her chance. This was my opportunity. I am the only woman in his life now. Like Nguyen said, "*She* was too needy."

"Let's have another drink, beautiful. We can look forward to better times ahead." He said, as he got up to order another bottle of wine.

"Sure, let's." I beamed.

The wound healed very quickly with Nguyen. The scar however, remains to serve a purpose. It is there to remind me about forgiveness. To forgive oneself is the ultimate success to the journey of self-discovery. If you can stop your thoughts spinning the hamster wheel, then you're off to a good start.

Self-respect. Loving thy self. If you love yourself, you do not need to seek love from others. Bullshit. We want our cake and to eat it too. Set boundaries, find what your values are and stick to them. Never bow down to have someone in your life, if they kick you to the curb, then walk away. The universe will push you off the wrong path beyond a shadow of doubt and set you on to the right one…eventually.

Loving relationships should include compromise, understanding, compassion, forgiveness, empathy, sex, balanced point of views, respect, effective communication, honesty, trust, direction and shedding the 'F' word, fear and introducing 'G' gratitude! Be grateful for what you have, and you will begin to see the bigger picture. You already have the right tools to work with.

Nevertheless, how do I apply all of these together? I was never good at swimming. I was so uncoordinated, I was afraid of drowning, how was I ever going to practice all the above at the same time? Keep practising…even if you have to develop your own swimming style!

Love yourself first before you go looking for someone else to fill your void. It is not rocket science. Otherwise, you will be forever chasing your tail attracting the same lesson over and over. Don't chase that pipedream that is not worthy of your love. Cupid had shot his arrow and it was headed right for me. Nguyen was everything I *thought* I had missed out on in life and that I now so deserved.

READ MORE
Paperback and kindle available now on Amazon

www.ingramcontent.com/pod-product-compliance
Lightning Source LLC
Chambersburg PA
CBHW050200120726
47903CB00002B/697